The Eddy problem

Have we discussed raccoons? Maybe so, because we've had several stories about Eddy the Rac. Remember Eddy? Slim and I saved him from some stray dogs when he was just a little shaver, and Slim kept him as a pet until he became such a pain in the neck everyone was glad to see him leave.

You might say that I'd helped raise Eddy. In some ways he was a nice little guy, but he was also a crook. See, one of the valuable lessons that Eddy taught me was that you should never trust Eddy. Behind that cute raccoon face and pleasant personality lurked the mind of a con artist. He could talk his way out of a jailhouse or a strait-jacket, and I must admit that even I had been victimized on a few occasions. Once or twice.

Once, and that was enough.

The Case of
the Tricky Trap

John R. Erickson

Illustrations by Gerald L. Holmes

PUFFIN BOOKS

PUFFIN BOOKS
Published by the Penguin Group
Penguin Young Readers Group, 345 Hudson Street, New York, New York 10014, U.S.A.
Penguin Group (Canada), 10 Alcorn Avenue, Toronto, Ontario, Canada M4V 3B2
(a division of Pearson Penguin Canada Inc.)
Penguin Books Ltd, 80 Strand, London WC2R 0RL, England
Penguin Ireland, 25 St Stephen's Green, Dublin 2, Ireland
(a division of Penguin Books Ltd)
Penguin Group (Australia), 250 Camberwell Road, Camberwell, Victoria 3124,
Australia (a division of Pearson Australia Group Pty Ltd)
Penguin Books India Pvt Ltd, 11 Community Centre, Panchsheel Park,
New Delhi - 110 017, India
Penguin Group (NZ), Cnr Airborne and Rosedale Roads, Albany,
Auckland 1310, New Zealand (a division of Pearson New Zealand Ltd)
Penguin Books (South Africa) (Pty) Ltd, 24 Sturdee Avenue, Rosebank,
Johannesburg 2196, South Africa

Registered Offices: Penguin Books Ltd, 80 Strand, London WC2R 0RL, England

Published simultaneously in the United States of America by Viking
and Puffin Books, divisions of Penguin Young Readers Group, 2005

3 5 7 9 10 8 6 4 2

Puffin Books ISBN 0-14-240325-3

Hank the Cowdog® is a registered trademark of John R. Erickson.

Printed in the United States of America

Dedicated to the memory of my grandmother,
Mable Sherman Curry

CONTENTS

Chapter One Salad Is Good for Dogs **1**

Chapter Two A Terrible Crime **11**

Chapter Three Dogs Should Never Eat Salad **21**

Chapter Four We Catch Something
in Our Trap **31**

Chapter Five Voices in the Night **42**

Chapter Six We Catch Something
Else in Our Trap **51**

Chapter Seven Wallace Sings a Dumb
Little Song **61**

Chapter Eight Ruined! **71**

Chapter Nine Buzzard Voodoo **83**

Chapter Ten Drover Disappears in the Night **93**

Chapter Eleven Eddy's Phony Helicopter **104**

Chapter Twelve Eddy Walks into My Trap **114**

CHAPTER ONE

Salad Is Good for Dogs

It's me again, Hank the Cowdog. The mystery began on a cold gloomy day in February, as I recall. March. No, it was February, because February begins with an *f* and ends in a *y*, and has twenty-three letters in between.

So, yes, it was a warm day in March. Drover and I had brought the ranch through another dark and dangerous night, had caught a few winks of sleep on our gunnysack beds, and had ventured out to do a routine patrol of ranch headquarters.

We were down by the corrals when I noticed several sprigs of winter grass that had popped out beneath the bottom board of the corral fence. Maybe you think that a few sprigs of greenery

1

should be no big deal, but it was. On our ranch, the first appearance of green grass is always a welcome sign, an omen that the dull brown grip of winter will soon fade into the soft days of spring.

I paused and sniffed the grass. Drover noticed, and seemed surprised. "What are you doing?"

"I'm stopping to smell the roses."

"Yeah, but it's just grass."

"Drover, today we have grass and tomorrow we'll have roses. This is the first green grass of the year and spring is on its way." He gave me a blank stare. "What's wrong with you? For three long months our world has been drab and brown, and here is a little splash of color. I'd think you'd be excited."

"Yeah, but I'm not."

I turned away from him and sniffed the greenery. "Who cares? I love the smell of this stuff. I mean, all winter we've lived with the smell of dust and dead leaves, but now . . ." I filled my lungs with the fragrance. "This is delicious! Wonderful! It smells almost good enough to eat."

I sniffed the grass again and all at once . . . well, the notion of eating some grass sounded pretty appealing, and you know what? Right then and there I nipped off the tender shoots of grass and swallowed them down.

Drover's eyes grew wide. "You ate grass?"

"Of course I did. For your information, it's not uncommon for dogs to eat grass, and do you know why?"

He shook his head. "I can't imagine."

"Then let me explain." I began pacing back and forth in front of him, as I often do when I'm forced to expand his tiny mind. "Number one, green grass cleans our teeth and freshens our breath. Number two, it's good for the digestion. Number three, after eating Co-op dog food all winter, we need some salad in our diet."

He stared at me. "Salad! I hate salad. It's for rabbits."

"Drover, what's good for rabbits is sometimes good for dogs. For your information, green grass contains many of the fillomens and mackerels that build healthy bones, hair, and muscle."

"You mean vitamins and minerals?"

"That's what I said."

"No, I think you said something about mack-erels."

I stopped pacing. "Drover, I said nothing about mackerels. Mackerels are fish. Fish live in water and they don't eat grass."

"Yeah, but . . ."

"I'm trying to give you a lesson on diet and nutrition. I'd appreciate it if you'd pay attention and stop talking about fish." I resumed my pacing. "Now, where was I?"

"Fillomens and mackerels."

"Yes, of course. It's common knowledge that Co-op dog food is made of sawdust and grease. Our people buy it because it's cheap, but it contains just the bare minimum of fillomens and mackerels to keep a dog alive. That's why we need salad in our diet from time to time."

"Yeah, but . . . eating grass?"

"Drover, there's more to this life than steak bones and meat. Doesn't your body ever cry out for something green and nourishing?"

He gave me a silly grin. "Nope. My body cries out for ice cream."

"Ice cream! No wonder you've turned out to be such a runt. Well, go ahead and be a stub-tailed, malnourished, half-starved little husk of a dog. I don't care. I'm going to eat my vegetables and then we'll see who's sorry."

"Fine with me."

Why do I bother trying to help Drover? I don't know. Experience has proven that it's a waste of time, but for some reason . . . oh well.

I had wasted my lecture on him, but that wasn't going to keep me from attending to my own dietary needs. The still, small voice inside my body had informed me that, after a long drab winter, I needed greenery in my diet. So I left Drover to dream of ice cream and proceeded to harvest every tender sprig of green grass I could find.

If he couldn't learn anything from my lectures, then maybe he could learn from the force of my example. That's the best way of teaching anyway, through example. The proof of the pudding is in the ice cream.

You know, ice cream did sound pretty good, but I was on a Nourishment Crusade and had to put all thoughts of ice cream out of my mind. Thirty minutes of careful grazing left me in great shape, spiritually and nutritionally, and by the time I had harvested about three hundred tender blades of grass, I was more convinced than ever that . . .

Well, that eating grass wasn't as exciting as you might think. I mean, a little grass goes a long way for a dog. Sure, I'd had a craving for the stuff, but you can't let those cravings get out of control. Moderation, that's the secret—moderation in all things.

Anyway, I took one last bite of grass, rolled it around in my mouth, and began to wonder how rabbits could stand to eat such garbage. I checked to make sure that Drover wasn't looking and spit it out. Yuck.

At that very moment, I heard the sound of an approaching vehicle. I looked up and saw Slim Chance, the ranch's hired hand, pulling up in front of the feed shed. And I knew it was exactly eight o'clock in the morning.

You're probably amazed that a dog would have such an uncanny sense of time. I mean, we don't carry watches or clocks, so how could I have known that it was exactly eight o'clock?

I'm sorry, but I can't reveal that information. See, the world is full of spies and enemy agents, and we have to be very careful about who knows the inner workings of the Security Division. Those guys never sleep, they never rest. Day and night, they're plotting mischief and looking for ways of hacking into our secret files. Why, if they knew all the formulas we use for keeping time . . .

Oh, what the heck, maybe it wouldn't hurt to give you a little peek. Okay, here we go. First off, we take precise measurements of the positions of the sun, the moon, and the planet Neeptide just before sunrise. Since the sun doesn't exist before sunrise, we drop it from the equation and mush on. We add the numbers together, divide by the number of legs on a spider (7.35), and multiply by three.

Why three? Well, it's a nice little number and we've always liked it. Furthermore, if you were taking a walk down Numbers Lane, three is the number you would meet between two and four.

If you do the math right, this complex equation will yield the exact time of day. But just in case we make some mistakes in our clackulations, we have ways of checking our work. For example, we have learned through careful observation that at eight o'clock in the wintertime, Slim Chance arrives at the feed shed. He has a coffee mug hooked onto the index finger of his right hand, his eyes are puffy, and he communicates in a language called Gruntlish.

In Gruntlish, *"Uh"* means "Good morning, dogs" and *"Uh grunt grunt uh"* means "Get out of the way." That's about the extent of his morning conversation. Anyway, our system of keeping time works to perfection and now you've had a little peek at our secret methods. When Slim parked the pickup in front of the feed shed, we knew it was exactly eight o'clock in the morning. What did we do with that information? Not much, actually, but we knew it wasn't raining or Tuesday.

Slim dragged himself out of the pickup, looked down at me with a pair of red-rimmed eyeballs, and said, *"Uh grunt grunt uh."* (Look one paragraph above for the translation.) He took a sip of coffee and threw open the shed door. For a moment, he stared inside, and then he muttered, *"Uh uh grunt uh grunt grunt grunt!"*

Drover turned a puzzled gaze on me. "What did he say?"

"I'm not sure. He's not usually so talkative in the morning. We've never had to translate such a long speech."

"Well, he looks kind of mad. Maybe he saw a mouse or something."

I studied Slim's face. Sure enough, he looked mad. "But why would he be mad about a mouse?"

"I don't know. Maybe a mouse ate his cheese."

I beamed him a glare. "Drover, Slim puts his cheese in the refrigerator, not in the feed shed. Feed in the feed shed, cheese in the refrigerator. Do you see a pattern here?"

"Yeah, but what about the pickles?"

"Pickles? Drover, pickles have nothing to do with anything."

"Well, they have to do with hamburgers, and I love hamburgers."

I shoved him aside. "Out of the way, and don't talk to me about pickles."

"Well, if you were a pickle, how would you feel if nobody ever talked about you?"

I ignored him. Did I have time to discuss pickles? No. Slim had seen something unusual in the feed shed, and had gone to the effort of muttering, *"Uh uh grunt uh grunt grunt grunt!"* We had some kind of problem on the ranch and I had to find out what it was. I marched up beside my cowboy friend and turned my gaze into the shed.

I was stunned, shocked. You see, Slim and I had just stumbled upon evidence of a terrible crime.

CHAPTER TWO

A Terrible Crime

A fifty-pound paper sack of turkey corn had been ripped open and the contents strewn across the floor of the shed.

What is "turkey corn"? Great question. See, Slim kept a sack of whole corn in the shed and every morning he threw some out on the ground for the wild turkeys. They're shameless moochers, you know, those turkeys. Throw out a little corn and they'll come running on their long gawky legs. After a few days of free corn, they won't even wait for you to throw it out. They'll run toward the sound of the pickup, and in fact that's what they were doing at that very moment.

I could hear them. Twenty-five head of turkey moochers were streaming toward the pickup, and had already started pushing and shoving, gobbling and squawking.

It was enough to throw Drover into a panic. He came running up beside me. "Hank, oh my gosh, there's a bunch of turkeys and I think . . ."

"Shhh. Hush. Drover, we've had a break-in."

He stared into the shed and let out a gasp. "Oh my gosh, look what the mice did!"

"Not mice, son. It's more serious than that. Unless I'm badly mistaken, we've got a professional burglar on the loose."

I pointed to some tracks near the door. Tracks tell it all, you know, and these resembled the little hand prints of a child. Drover's eyes bugged out. "Oh my gosh, Baby Molly's been stealing corn!"

I let out a groan. "Drover, please. Those are raccoon tracks, and unless I'm badly mistaken, they were left by a coon."

At that very moment, Slim began speaking in English. "Dadgum coons! Look at that mess. If we don't get 'em stopped, they'll tear open every sack in the shed." He heaved a sigh and scowled at the old wooden door. If you recall, it was warped at the bottom, so that a coon or even a dog could slither inside. "One of these days, somebody needs to fix that door."

Yes? I waited for him to volunteer for the job—a job, by the way, that had needed doing for years.

"But not today, I ain't got time." He hitched up his jeans and grinned. "But by grabs, I've got time to set a trap for the little feller. Heh. I'll fix him."

I stared at him in disbelief. I don't want to seem critical of my people, but this struck me as a bit nutty. The door was broken, so he was going to fix the *coon*? Did that make sense? No, but it was typical of Slim's method of approaching any kind of construction work or repairs.

Ignore the door and fix the coon. Oh, brother.

Moments later, Slim had abandoned his plans for loading up sacks of feed and was driving up to the machine shed. (He didn't invite us dogs to ride, so we had to escort the pickup.) He parked near the west side of the shed and waded out into some dead weeds that came up past his knees. This was the place where Slim and Loper stored various odds and ends that were left over from their work projects. There was a pile of old lumber, a pile of welding scraps, a pile of rotten cedar posts, and a pile of junk parts from the tractor and hay baler. It was meant to be a "temporary" junkyard, only the stuff had been there for years and had ceased being "temporary" a long time ago.

I'll say no more about them being careless and sloppy. They never listen to their dogs anyway.

Slim prowled through the piles of junk and stomped down weeds until at last he pointed toward something that appeared to be a wire cage. "There she is." He grinned. "That's my live-trap, dogs. I haven't used it in quite a spell."

Yes, I could believe that he hadn't used it in "quite a spell." You could hardly even see it for all the weeds that had grown up around it. After considerable lifting, pushing, heaving, and grunting, he got the thing out of the weeds, and Drover and I were able to take a closer look at this so-called live-trap.

For the most part, it was just a cage made of welded rods and covered with mesh wire, maybe four feet long, two feet wide, and three feet high. The thing that made it different from a cage was that on one end, it had a trapdoor that would slam shut if someone or something crawled inside and stepped on the trigger mechanism.

That sounds complicated, doesn't it? It wasn't. If it had been complicated, Slim couldn't have built it. I'm sorry to put it that way, but it's the truth.

Slim dragged it to the rear of the pickup and managed to heave it up into the bed. He was in a better mood by this time, and he even invited us dogs to ride in the cab down to the feed shed.

I took my usual Shotgun Position on the right side of the pickup. As you may know, we dogs love to hang our heads out an open window. It gives us a clear view of the road ahead and, well, there's just something invigorating about fresh air. We love that stream of fresh air that blows across our tongues and causes our ears to stand out behind us.

Unfortunately, the window was rolled up (the morning was a little frosty), and right away I began to notice . . . well, stale air. Slim's pickup had a distinctive smell, don't you see, and it was never what you would call pleasant. But now it seemed even worse than usual. Old pipe tobacco. Stale coffee. Dirty socks. Cowboy sweat.

And Drover. He was sitting on the seat beside me. "Drover, when was the last time you took a bath?"

"Well, let me think. I can't remember. You know I hate water."

"Yes, I'm aware of that. Look, I don't mean to sound critical, but something really stinks in this pickup. It's making me ill."

"Maybe it was all that grass you ate."

I roasted him with a glare. "Don't be ridicu-

lous, and don't try to change the subject. Take a bath sometime or you might end up with no friends." I turned my gaze back to the . . . boy, I sure wished the window was open. I needed some fresh air. And it didn't help that Slim seemed to be hitting every bump in the road. How many bumps could you find in a short stretch of road between the machine shed and the feed shed? Ten thousand, and he hit every one of them dead-center.

As we bounced down the hill in front of the house, I noticed that my head was beginning to sink and my eyes seemed to have . . . well, glazed over, shall we say. And the air had become so oppressive that I could hardly breathe. The cab smelled awful, like the dark smoke coming off a pile of burning tires.

I shot a glance at Slim. He was grinning and poking along at about three miles an hour, lost in thoughts of his next big adventure, catching a live raccoon in his fleabag trap. *Could we hurry up?* I mean, it was nice that he had let us dogs ride in the pickup with him, but for crying out loud . . .

Hot waves began washing across my face. I was smothering! My tongue was dripping like a leaky faucet. And my stomach . . . something was going on down there and it wasn't good news.

Something very bad was happening in the deep caverns of my . . .

I stared at the road ahead and tried to concentrate on pleasant thoughts: sunshine, spring flowers, green grass . . . oops, that was exactly the wrong topic to be thinking about, because . . .

Listen, we need to talk about green grass. Remember my lecture to Drover about the importance of salad in a dog's diet, and how grass is good for the digestion? It had sounded good at the time, and I had spoken those words with the greatest of sincerity, no kidding, but I was beginning to suspect that . . . how can I say this? Okay, let's try another approach. In the Great Game of Life, we have our facts that have been proven through years of experience and those facts that are still . . . uh . . . theoretical. The theoretical facts sound good, and sometimes they even sound great, but they haven't been submitted to rigorous testing.

See, we knew for a fact that dogs sometimes get an irrational craving for green grass. What we didn't know, what we couldn't have known, was . . . well, what might happen if a dog not only ate a few sprigs of grass, but maybe ate a whole bunch of it. A gallon. A bushel. Half a ton.

We had no test data to show what might

happen to a dog who wolfed down two tons of green grass, but our internal instruments were beginning to suggest . . .

I swallowed hard and stared at the road ahead. I was panting and my tongue continued to drip. The air inside the cab had turned hot and putrid. I really needed to, uh, step outside for a moment, but Slim was still poking along, as slow as a . . .

Uh-oh. I felt this . . . this creepy feeling in the dark depths of my innards, as though a mysterious hand had reached inside me, had closed its deadly grip around my stomach, and had begun . . .

All at once my head began moving up and down, and I heard this . . . this really weird sound that seemed to be coming from . . . well, from my own body and soul. UMP. UMP. It wasn't a happy sound or the kind of sound a dog would want to make inside the closed cab of a pickup that smelled like . . .

And suddenly I knew that my life had been seized by Unseen Forces. See, that business of my head moving up and down . . . I wasn't in control of it. It wasn't coming from my own free will. Some evil force had climbed inside my body, had taken command of all my Vital Plumbing Functions, and . . .

The pickup came to a sudden stop and I went crashing nose-first into the dashboard. I turned my soggy eyes toward Slim and saw that . . . well, that he had melted into a blob of bacon fat. Honest. His face was wavy and fuzzy . . . UMP, UMP . . . and, gee, my head was moving up and down again . . .

"Hank, if you barf in my pickup . . . !"

After that, everything became a blur.

CHAPTER THREE

Dogs Should Never Eat Salad

Where were we? Oh yes, hauling Slim's live-trap down to the feed shed. No problems there. The mission was a complete success. We hauled the trap down to the feed shed. Slim backed the pickup to the door and we began . . .

Wait a second. We've skipped over a few details. To be honest, I'd rather not talk about them, but I guess we have to. You already know, don't you?

It wasn't a pleasant experience, but maybe we can wring a few Life Lessons out of the dishrag of . . . something.

Let's get it over with. Remember those mysterious convulsions that were causing my head to move up and down? We thought my stomach had been taken over by the Evil Gremlins, right? Well, this will come as a surprise, but those forces had been produced by my own body. I had become a sick dog.

What could have brought on this mysterious illness? Well, riding in a closed pickup was a big part of it. And being bounced around on a rough road. And don't forget that it was flu season. I mean, we'd heard reports that dogs all over Texas were dropping like flies. No kidding.

Okay, the green grass. If you recall, we'd gotten some bogus information suggesting that green grass is good for a dog's digestion. Ha! Rubbish. I don't know who puts out such screwball information or who would be dumb enough to . . .

Wait. That report had come from Drover, right? I'm almost sure it had. Let me think back and try to remember our conversation exactly. As I recall, Drover had tried to convince me that eating grass is something a dog should do. How did he put it? Salad. He said that green grass is actually a form of salad and that dogs need salad as part of their overall dietary so-forth.

And as I recall, I laughed and scoffed at the idea. I mean, what a joke. A dog eating grass! Ha! But on the other hand, I had no wish to hurt the little guy's feelings. He tries to be helpful, you know, and I sure didn't want to, uh, crush his spirit, let us say.

So what's a dog supposed to do, tell his friend that he's come up with a crazy idea? Laugh in his face? A lot of dogs would have done that, but, well, there's a part of me that's very sensitive to the, uh, feelings of others. No kidding.

So I took a Higher Road, so to speak, and . . . well, you know the rest. I ate a bunch of grass. And let's talk about that. Grass is for RABBITS. Grass is for cows, horses, sheep, and other forms of life that are too dumb to eat proper food. The bottom line here is that *dogs should never eat salad or grass.*

But I did it anyway—for Drover. Was my sacrifice worth the price I had to pay? I'm not sure. It certainly got Slim stirred up. I mean, on an ordinary morning he's not what you would call electric, but fellers, when he saw my head moving up and down, and heard those horrible sounds coming from the depths of my inner bean, he went electric.

In the space of a few seconds, he slammed on the brakes, jerked the door open, and chunked me out of the cab. And then he said . . . this kind of hurt my feelings . . . he said, "Hank, you've got no more class than a sack full of turnips!"

What did *class* have to do with it? Hey, what did he want me to do, sit there like a nice little doggie and die of Salad Poisoning? Ha. He could forget that.

Oh, and he had one more hateful remark. I couldn't believe this part. He said, and this is a direct quote, he said, "Hank, do me a favor. When you throw up, don't eat it again. Bozo."

Well, I had never been so insulted! The very idea, him thinking that I might . . . I held my head at a proud angle and beamed him a look of righteous . . . UMP, UMP . . . that is, all at once the gravitational force of the earth pulled my nose toward the ground. My head moved up and down three times, as unseen forces activated powerful pumps in my gizzardly depths. And then . . .

Anyway, the toxic particles returned to the embrace of Mother Earth, shall we say, and suddenly I felt that a heavy burden had been lifted from my shoulders. From my stomach. I felt a hundred percent better, is the point, and I turned a righteous glare at Slim, who was driving away.

"And for your information, pal, I wouldn't even *think* about eating it again! What do you think I am, a moron?"

There! He didn't hear me, but that was okay. I had needed to express my feelings of outrage, and I'd done it.

At that point, I looked down at the ground and saw . . . hmmm. Sprigs of green parsley floating in a French sauce. Hmmmm. You know, some experts claim that parsley is actually good for dogs, and all at once . . . never mind.

The impointant poink is that I had made a noble sacrifice to spare little Drover from embarrassment and humiliation. Yes, I had paid a price for my good deed. Slim had thrown me out of the pickup and had mocked me in my time of weakness, but in the Security Business, we have learned that virus is its own reward.

Virtue, that is. Virtue is its own reward and sometimes that's all we get.

Now, where were we before this crisis began? Oh yes, the trap. I didn't help Slim set his trap in the feed shed, not after he'd insulted me and wounded my spiritual so-forth. Any man who would insult a loyal, hard-working dog in a time of trouble didn't deserve to be helped.

He deserved to be shunned and ignored, and that's what I did. For the rest of the day, I stayed away from him. I didn't even help him feed the cows. Anytime he came close to me, I turned my back on him, rolled my eyes up to the heavens, and assumed a posture we call "Martyrs and Saints."

The whole purpose of Martyrs and Saints is to remind the offending party (Slim) of all the saints and loyal dogs of long ago, whose good deeds and sacrifices had left a shining example for those who followed.

Did it work on Slim? We'll never know. He's a hammerhead, very stubborn and not too bright, and I'm sure the deeper messages were lost on him. But he knew that I was torqued. It didn't take a genius to figure that out.

Around sundown, after putting in an exhausting day of doing Martyrs and Saints, I returned to my office on the twelfth floor of the Security Division's Vast Office Complex. Okay, my office was under the gas tanks, but who's impressed if you tell 'em your office is under a couple of five-hundred-gallon fuel tanks? Nobody.

I breezed into the office, checked the stack of mail on my desk, and noticed that Drover was already there, gawking at me.

I gave him a stiff nod. "Oh, so it's you."

"Thanks, me too. How was your day?"

"My day was . . ." I allowed my gaze to drift around, then I dropped it on him like a hammer.

"Drover, I've decided I'm going to forgive you."

"Oh, good. Thanks." There was a moment of silence. "What did I do?"

"You stood by and watched while I consumed toxic quantities of green grass."

"Yeah, but . . ."

"It made me sick. I could have died."

"Yeah, but . . ."

"Drover, I thought we were comrades. Friends. Partners in the Journey of Life."

"Yeah, but you said . . ."

"I know what I said, but you stood there and let me say it."

His head began to sink. "Well . . ."

"Drover, dogs were never meant to eat grass or salad or anything a rabbit would eat. You knew that, didn't you?"

"Yeah, and I tried to warn you, but you never listen."

I looked down at him and shook my head. "See? You're turning this thing around and trying to blame *me* for it."

"Well, you ate it!"

"There you go again. You're accusing me of eating the very grass that made me sick? Is that what you're telling this court?"

"Yeah, and it's the truth."

I paced a few steps away, lost in deep thoughts. "Drover, there are many shades of truth. Our task here is to find the right shade that will allow you to take some responsibility for my own actions."

"You mean . . ."

I whirled around and faced him. "Yes! Admit that mistakes were made, apologize for my actions, and let's get on with our lives."

He sniffed his nose and wiped a tear from his eye. "Well, okay. I'm sorry you made such a dumb mistake."

"You really mean that?" He nodded. I rushed to his side and extended the Paw of Friendship. "Good for you. Here, let's shake on it. Drover, it takes a real dog to do what you just did."

"Well, I've always tried to be real."

"And you've succeeded. I'm proud of you, son. Don't you feel better already?"

He worked up a smile. "Yeah, but you know, I never felt all that bad to start with. You're the one who threw up."

"Hmmm, good point. But you're feeling better about that?"

"Oh yeah, I thought it was funny as heck."

I stared at him. "What?"

"I didn't say anything."

"You did say something. Did you say it was funny as heck?"

"No, I said . . . I said, I sure like this gunny sack."

"Oh. Yes, it's nice, isn't it?"

"Great sack."

This had turned into kind of a touching moment. I mean, we had worked our way through a crisis situation and had confronted Drover's problems head-on. I placed a paw on his shoulder and gazed up at the darkening sky. "You know, son, in this crazy business, all we have is us, ourselves."

"Well, we've got fleas."

"I know, but at a deeper level, it's just you and me against the forces of evil. The only thing that keeps us going is . . . the quality of our minds." Drover began to cough. "Did you choke on something?"

"Yeah, it's hard to swallow."

"Beware of swallowing, son. Don't forget, that's how you got us into this mess in the first place."

And with that, we shut off the lights, turned off all our communications systems, and prepared for some well-deserved sleep.

CHAPTER FOUR

We Catch Something in Our Trap

It must have been sometime in the middle of the night. I awoke with a jolt and sat up. "Drover, I hate to disturb you, but I just thought of something."

In the darkness, I heard his voice. "Thought bought murgle wump watermelon."

"Are you awake?"

"Rumple ragamuffin."

"Slim set a live-trap in the feed shed, remember?"

"Remember December hopalong horse feathers."

"Drover, one of us needs to check the trap. I was wondering if you might like to volunteer." I lifted my ears, waiting for his answer. I heard grunts and squeaks. "Drover, this could be a very smart career move. It would look good on your résumé. Think of it: trap-checking on a dark lonely night. What do you say?"

"Murgle skiffer pork chop, buzz blop buggy bumpers."

I heaved a sigh, jacked myself up to a standing position, and gazed down at his twitching carcass. "Look, I'm not going to argue about this all night. Do you want the job or not?"

"Honk wheeze whiffle."

"Fine, I'll do it myself. Just tell me again how the trap works. I don't want to walk into this thing blind."

"Wheezle whickerbill soap suds."

"On second thought, just skip it."

I whirled around and marched out of the office. As I began my trek to the feed shed, I found myself thinking about this latest conversation with my assistant. It's been said that the sleeping mind sometimes reveals deep thoughts that disguise themselves as nonsense. Was it possible that Drover's slumbering mind had tried to communicate some hidden message? I probed my memory and pulled up a transcript of his mutterings:

1. Rumple ragamuffin.
2. Hopalong horse feathers.

3. Buzz blop buggy bumpers.
4. Honk wheeze whiffle.
5. Wheezle whickerbill soap suds.

Was there some thread that ran through these beads of nonsense and gave them a shape that wasn't obvious at first glance? The more I thought about it, the more convinced I became that, yes, something profound was going on here. For example, did you notice that he tended to repeat certain sounds? Rumple ragamuffin, buzz blop buggy bumpers, and so forth. That had to mean something, didn't it?

And look at the wide variety of subjects he'd covered in the space of just a few seconds: watermelons, ragamuffins, horse feathers, whiffles, whickerbills, buggy bumpers, and soap suds. That was really amazing. I mean, when he was awake, Drover never talked about those subjects, so the clues were beginning to suggest that he had a secret life that he'd never shared with the rest of us.

I tried to imagine the fantasy world that Drover had invented for himself. It was a place where horses had feathers, ragamuffins wore rumpled suits, buggies had bumpers, and whickerbills ate soap suds. Now, if I could just

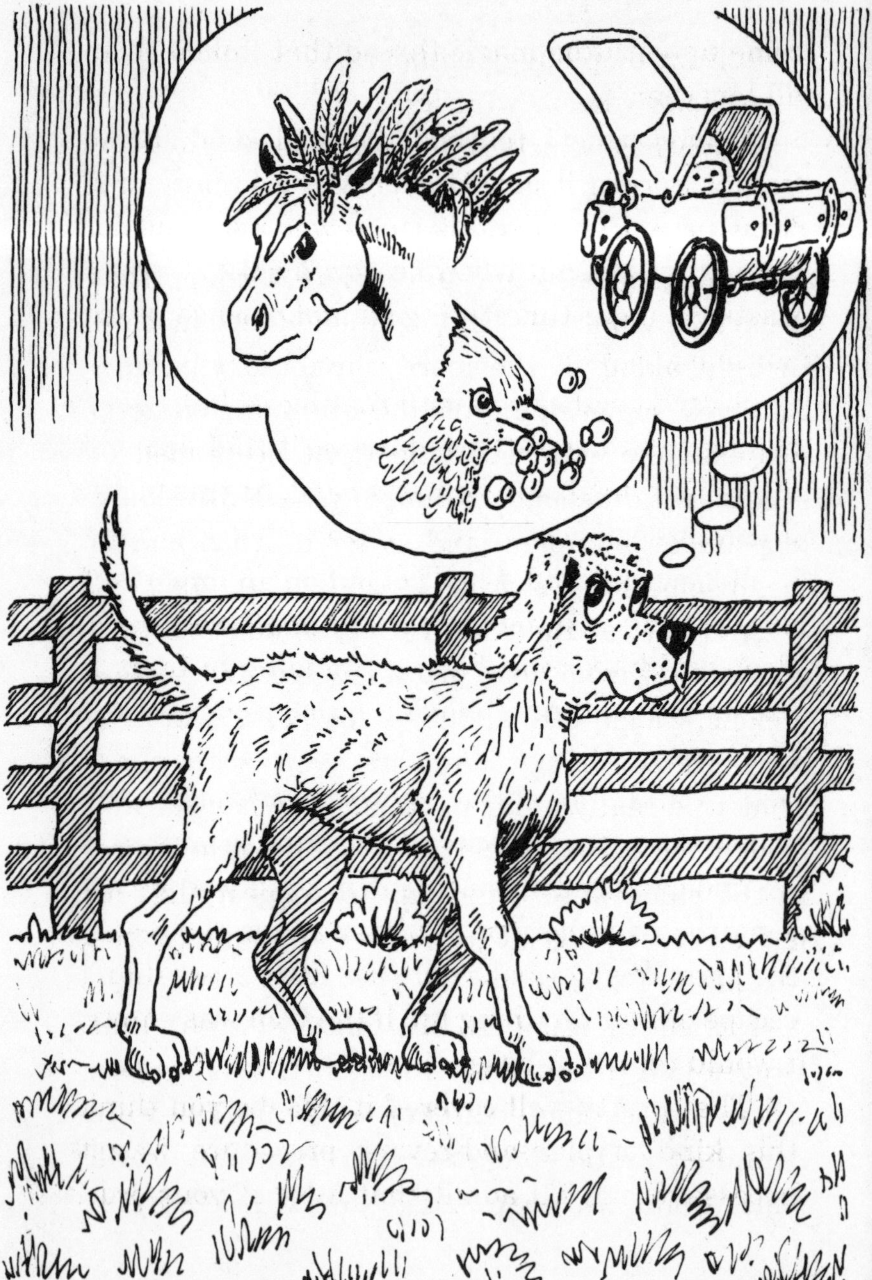

come up with the magic thread that linked them all together . . .

By the time I reached the feed shed, I had finally worked it out. Drover was a lunatic, and what he muttered in his sleep was even nuttier than what he said when he was awake. I would waste no more time trying to make sense of his nonsense.

Sorry to bother you with that mess, but I keep hoping that one of these days we'll find signs of intelligent life inside Drover's head. At this point, it doesn't look good.

But never mind. I had set out on an important mission and nothing Drover had muttered in his sleep could keep me from it. Standing in front of the feed-shed door, I made a quick review of my objectives.

I would enter the structure through the warped door and check out the trap situation. If we had captured a thieving raccoon, I would post a guard and remain on station through the rest of the night, just to make sure the little creep didn't escape or tear anything up. If the trap was empty, I would return to base.

That pretty well covered it. Maybe you think this kind of plan-and-review procedure wasn't necessary, and I'll admit that a lot of your ordinary dogs wouldn't have bothered to go through a checklist. But we do things a little differently in our Security Division. See, ninety percent of mission failures are caused by dumb little mistakes: inadequate planning, poor concentration, and . . .

What was the other one? I don't remember, but it was a dandy. Oh well, two reasons for mission failure are plenty. After all, it only takes one dumb mistake to wreck a mission.

Where were we? Oh yes, poor concentration. The main difference between your Heads of Ranch Security and your ordinary run of ranch mutts is . . . I can't remember that one either, so let's skip it and get on with the mission.

Okay, I was ready. I squared my enormous soldiers . . . shoulders, let us say, and took a big gulp of air. I would need that air when I got inside. Air is extremely important, and ninety percent of mission failures are caused by a lack of air.

I went into the Crouch Position, inched toward the warped section of the shed door, and allowed my nose and head to penetrate inside. There, I switched over to Infrared Vision and scoped out the interior of the shed. I saw sacks of feed, fifteen bales of prairie hay, and Slim's live-trap.

Twisting the knobs on the Night Scope, I

brought the trap into focus and scoped it out from one end to the other. At first the trap appeared to be empty, but closer inspection revealed that it was . . . well, empty. Phooey. Either the burglar hadn't shown up or the trap wasn't working. I had no choice but to go closer and check it out.

I slithered my way inside the shed and marched straight to the trap. It was still empty, so that confirmed our first observation. The next question was, why? I ran my gaze over the trap, studying the mechanical components and the trigger mechanism.

It seemed pretty obvious that Slim had muffed the job of setting the trap. I mean, it was a simple device and any dog could have set the thing right, but Slim had tried it on his own, without a dog around to keep an eye on things. So what could you expect? A typical cowboy job, slap-dash and half-done. I would have to enter the trap myself and conduct a complete and thorough inspection. My report would send shock waves all the way to the top, but that was too bad. It couldn't be helped. Incompetence must be explored.

Exposed, let us say. Incompetence must be exposed.

I crept inside the trap and started Dictation. "March 12, 2:47 am. What we are looking at is a crude live-trap, made by a cowboy welder. Over here, we have the linkage mechanism made of metal rebar. The linkage runs from the trapdoor on the anterior side and connects to the trigger mechanism inside the trap.

"You'll notice that the trigger is made of an old license plate. It seems clear that the failure occurred because the trap wasn't properly armed and set. To prove this, we will now set a paw upon the trigger plate . . . "

SLAM!

Huh?

Okay, remember that report I was dictating? We've decided not to use it. It contained some . . . some faulty data. See, we were operating on the assumption that the Trap Personnel had failed to arm the trap, but after testing the systems, we . . . uh . . . found this to not be the case, so to speak.

We . . . we got caught in our own trap, you might say. Ha ha. No problem. Anyway, all systems seemed to be functioning, and testing the systems had been the whole purpose of the mission, right? It was no big deal and it could have happened to anyone.

But it would become a bigger deal at eight o'clock. I knew what was coming and stayed up most of the night rehearsing my story:

"Slim, I know what you're thinking: 'Hank blundered into the trap and set it off.' Am I right? But let me assure you that it's not that simple. See, I wasn't with you yesterday when you set the trap and, well, I felt some concern . . . a great concern, actually, that maybe it wasn't properly armed.

"See, I'm the kind of dog who cares about these things, so I . . . I couldn't sleep at all, Slim, no kidding, I mean you talk about a dog who really *cares* about his people! That's me. Anyway, I felt it was my duty to, you know, check out all the systems. And, hey, what do you know? I, uh, trapped myself. Ha ha."

At eight o'clock, the shed door opened and Slim stepped inside. There was no Ha Ha in his face. I recognized several of his usual morning characteristics: a mug of coffee hooked onto his index finger, soggy red-rimmed eyes, a pillow crease on his right cheek, and a humorless slash of a mouth.

He stared at me and I stared at him. I tried to squeeze up a smile and began tapping out a slow rhythm with my tail. Tap, tap, tap. He mumbled, "Hank, what in the cat hair are you doing in my coon trap?"

Well, I . . . it was hard to explain. No, it was

39

impossible to explain with him standing there, glaring at me with those horrible bloodshot eyes. No wonder he was still a bachelor. Any woman who saw that face in the morning would call the police.

But... wait. He took a sip of coffee and smiled. Then he started laughing. The frost and ice in his face melted into something warmer and kinder, and I began to feel better about this deal.

"Hank, you are such a birdbrain, and my life would be so boring if someone was to wring your neck. Well, let's get you out of there."

Oh, happy day! He wasn't going to wring my neck or leave me inside the trap for weeks and weeks! He opened the door and let me out. Oh, freedom and friendship! I leaped into the middle of him with such an awesome display of love and devotion that it knocked him into a bale of hay and he fell over backward.

I didn't care. I licked his face with the kind of vigor unknown to ordinary dogs. We were pals again, that's all that mattered. He understood that I'd been trying to do my job, and I understood that his calling me "birdbrain" had been a careless slip the tongue. The old wounds were healed and all was right with the world. Yippee!

"Quit." He pushed me away and rose to his

feet. "Hank, there's just one thing I want to say. See that trap yonder? It's for a *raccoon*."

Right, I understood that.

"And I want you to promise me on your Doggie Word of Honor that you won't spring my trap again."

Oh, yes sir! That was a promise. On my honor. Five long hours inside the stupid trap had made me an older dog, a wiser dog in every way. I'd had time to review my life and think about my priorities, set goals and plan for the future, and he had my solemn oath that I would never pull that stunt again. Never.

As you can see, our clean slate was starting off on the right foot.

CHAPTER FIVE

Voices in the Night

I stood nearby and watched as Slim reset the trap. He propped the trapdoor open with a piece of lumber and set the trigger mechanism. I was impressed. He did everything right. Even I couldn't have done better. Then he went outside to his pickup and came back with . . . what was that?

He beamed a grin at me and held up a tin can. "The raccoons around here seem to like corn, so Tonight's Special is going to be canned corn. This'll work, pooch."

He gave me a wink, pulled a can opener out of his jacket pocket, and cranked it until the lid fell off the can. Then he got down on his knees and eased the can of corn onto the trigger plate. Gee, that was a pretty sneaky idea. Instead of letting the thief tear up sacks of feed, we were going to draw him into the trap with bait.

Heh heh. Old Slim and I made a pretty awesome team, don't you think? You bet. On our ranch, a thieving raccoon didn't have much of a chance.

Have we discussed raccoons? Maybe so, because we've had several stories about Eddy the Rac. Remember Eddy? Slim and I saved him from some stray dogs when he was just a little shaver, and Slim kept him as a pet until he became such a pain in the neck, everyone was glad to see him leave.

You might say that I'd helped raise Eddy. In some ways he was a nice little guy, but he was also a crook. See, one of the valuable lessons Eddy had taught me was that you should never trust Eddy. Behind that cute raccoon face and pleasant personality lurked the mind of a con artist. He could talk his way out of a jailhouse or a straitjacket, and I must admit that even I had been victimized on a few occasions. Once or twice.

Once, and that was enough. Do you remember that scam? It was one of Eddy's famous "deals," see. Slim had shut him up for the night inside a rabbit cage and Eddy wanted out. Eddy always

wanted out. Anyway, he . . . this is embarrassing
. . . the little sneak convinced me that the cage
was actually an elevator, and that if I opened the
door and crawled inside, we could . . . well, go for
a ride up to the third floor.

I'm not going to tell you the rest of it. It's still
too painful, too embarrassing. I thought the
wound had healed, but it hasn't.

Okay, I'll tell you, if you'll swear not to laugh
or tell anyone else. Promise? Here's the scoop.

I, being a trusting soul, opened the door and
crawled inside, while Eddy vanished like a puff of
smoke, and come morning, guess who was stuck
inside the rabbit cage? Me. For days I had to
endure the mockery and ridicule of the small
minds on this ranch, Slim and Loper. Oh, they
thought it was hilarious! Hank spending the
night in the rabbit cage.

It wasn't hilarious. It was one of the most
humiliating experiences of my entire career,
burned into my memory with a hot iron. So now
you know the story on Eddy: a happy little guy
who could be counted on to get a dog into trouble.
Eddy was Bad News, period.

Was he the one who'd wrecked the feed shed?
We had found coon tracks, but no information
that actually linked him to the crime. Maybe we

were gunning for Eddy or for some of his pals—it didn't matter to me. Justice would be done. The thieves would be hauled away from ranch headquarters and dumped off in another location. If Eddy was the culprit, we would catch him and he would have to pay the price.

See, when it comes to busting crooks and solving cases, the Head of Ranch Security has no friends.

Anyway, that's the file on Eddy the Rac . . . well, part of the file. There's more but I'm not at liberty to discuss it. The rest of his file is still classified and that information won't be released for twenty-five or thirty years.

Where were we? As you can see, just talking about Eddy gets me worked up, the little scrounge. Oh yes, we had reset and baited the trap. Slim loaded twenty sacks of feed onto the back of the pickup and we went on with our daily routine, feeding the cows in all seven pastures. Everything went fine and we returned to ranch headquarters late that afternoon.

Did you happen to notice that I didn't mention Drover? The reason is that he went AWOL and spent the entire day spouting roots on his gunnysack bed. No kidding. I mean, what kind of dog sleeps all night and then all day?

Drover, that's who, but don't think that he got by with it. I wrote him up, gave him seven Chicken Marks for laziness and disgraceful behavior. Oh, he sniffled and cried, but I didn't care. He'd brought it upon himself.

You know what he did then? He went back to sleep! Oh well.

Anyway, darkness fell. It happens every day after the sun goes down, don't you see, and we think there's some connection: sun goes down, it gets dark. I was too restless to sleep. I mean, I couldn't take my mind off that trap. I paced around the office and tried to think of something else, but my ears kept straining to hear something down at the feed shed.

This was exactly the wrong approach, and I knew it. When we're deeply involved in a stakeout or a trap situation, the best course of action is to forget about it, leave it alone, let things happen in their own time. Remember the wise old saying? "A potted watch never boils." It's true, very true. Potted watches *never* boil.

What exactly is a potted watch? I've wondered about that. I guess you could plant one in a flower pot and . . . I don't know, give it water and plenty of sunshine. It seems odd that anyone would want to plant a watch in a flower pot, but the impartant poink is that when you pot a watch, it never boils.

On the other hand, if you throw an unpotted watch into a pan of boiling water, it will boil every time. Thus, the wise old saying is wise and true.

It's kind of impressive that a dog would know so many wise old sayings, isn't it? I agree, and thanks for noticing. Yes, those wise old sayings have helped me solve many a case. Unfortunately, the wise old sayings weren't helping me much on this particular night, as I paced and fumed and waited to hear some action from our trap in the feed shed. The hours dragged by, then—it must have been around three o'clock in the morning— I heard several odd rustling sounds coming from the general vaccination of the feed shed . . . the general *vicinity*, let us say. Rustling sounds, then voices.

Maybe I should have stayed out of it and let events take their course, but . . . well, you know me. I'm not the kind of dog who's good about waiting. Give me action! So it will come as no surprise that I shifted into Stealthy Crouch Mode and began creeping toward the feed shed.

It puzzled me that I had heard *voices*. See, by its very nature, the word "voices" suggests more

than one suspect. It's puerile . . . purple . . . pureed
. . . phooey. "Voices" is the *plural* of "voice," don't
you see, and you can't have two voices coming
from one suspect. Well, I guess you could if some
nut was down there putting on a show and doing
different voices, but that wasn't likely.

So, yes, this gave me an important clue in the
case. We had multiple suspects. If that was Eddy
down there, he'd brought some of his buddies
with him.

This . . . uh . . . caused me some concern. I
mean, Eddy had these two cousins, Harley and
Choo Choo, big guys who thought they were pretty
tough, and the bad news was that they *were* tough.
I'd tangled with them a couple of times and . . .
well, those hadn't been happy experiences for me.

Maybe I should have dropped the case and
gone to bed, but I crept on through the inky black
inkiness of the darkness. Fifty feet from the shed,
I stopped and listened. I could hear the voices
clearly now.

"Junior, hush. I know what I'm a-doing."

"Y-yeah, b-but P-p-pa . . ."

"Quit talking so loud! There's dogs around
here and we don't want to get 'em stirred up. The
last thing we need is a bunch of noisy yapping
dogs, so hush up."

"Y-yeah, b-but P-p-pa, I d-don't think y-you ought to g-g-go in that sh-shed."

"Why? Junior, we've been working these roads and ditches for two weeks, and what did we get?"

"W-w-well, one l-l-little m-mouse, mouse."

"That's right. Two weeks' work for one sorry little mouse. Son, two buzzards can't stay in business like that. We need grub, serious grub."

"Y-y-yeah, b-but the shed's d-d-dark and s-s-s-spooky."

"Spooky? I'll show you spooky! Lookie here at my ribs sticking out like an I-don't-know-what. Son, your poor old daddy is wasting away and I'm going into that shed to look for grub."

"W-w-well, okay, b-but watch out f-f-for g-g-g-ghosts."

"Ghosts? Junior, I am a ghost! I'm a ghost of my former self. I'm a ghost of a healthy well-fed American buzzard. Now, you stand guard in this tree. I'm a-going inside."

"Okay, P-p-pa. W-w-w-whatever y-you s-s-say."

Did you hear that conversation? You probably think it came from a gang of thuggish raccoons, right? Well, I've got a big surprise. Those voices came from Wallace and Junior the buzzards!

CHAPTER SIX

We Catch Something Else in Our Trap

<hr />

Well, this case had certainly taken an interesting twist. Who would have ever suspected that our barn-wreckers would turn out to be a couple of half-starved buzzards? Not me. I was astounded.

I mean, we'd found coon tracks around the shed yesterday morning, and most of the time a guy assumes that coon tracks were left by coons, right? It was very confusing and it took me a minute to figure it out.

Special shoes. Wallace and Junior had equipped themselves with special shoes that left the tracks of a raccoon. Very clever. I never would have thought that Wallace and Junior would be devious enough to pull such a stunt, but here was the proof staring me in the face. When you find coon tracks and no coon, there's something fishy going on.

I took up a position about twenty feet from the door of the shed and hid in the shadows. I heard the rustle of wings and a moment later, Wallace crash-landed in front of the shed. He hoisted himself off the ground, looked up in a tree nearby, and said, "Shhhh!"

A voice in the darkness said, "D-d-don't sh-shush me. I d-d-didn't m-make a s-s-sound."

"Well, shush anyway."

Wallace rolled his head around, looking in all directions. Then he started tip-toeing toward the shed door. He stopped, glanced around again, and stuck his head inside. There he stood, all bent over with his tail feathers pointing toward the moon. I was sorely tempted to rush forward and take a bite out of his tail section (wouldn't that have been a riot?), but I imposed discipline upon myself and held my position.

We needed to gather some more evidence in this case before we sent in the Special Crimes Unit. If we gave Wallace plenty of rope, he would eventually hang out his laundry.

Once again, I heard Junior's voice. "P-p-pa? W-w-what do you s-s-see?"

Wallace's head emerged. "Junior, how do you feel about corn?"

"C-c-c-corn? Y-you m-mean like c-c-corn f-f-f-flakes, corn flakes?"

"No sir, I don't mean cornflakes. I mean corn."

"A s-s-sack of c-c-corn?"

Wallace stuck his head inside and pulled it out again. "It's in a can, a tin can. Canned corn is what we're talking about here."

"Oh g-g-gosh. Is the c-c-can opened?"

Wallace scowled. "Junior, we can stand here and play twenty questions or we can eat a can of corn, but we can't do both. I didn't write the menu."

"W-w-well, I'm n-n-not too c-c-crazy about c-c-c-corn, P-pa."

"Fine with me, I didn't want to share anyway. You stay up there and dream about prime rib, I'm going to eat some corn." Wallace whirled around and started crawling into the shed. But then he backed out and looked up into the tree. "But don't be whining about how you ain't had anything to eat in two weeks. I can't stand a whiny buzzard."

"Uh uh okay, P-p-pa."

Wallace wiggled and squeezed himself through the door, and disappeared inside. Well! This case was moving right along. In two minutes, we would have us a live buzzard inside the trap. I would stand guard and at eight o'clock in the morning, Slim would arrive and I would hand over the prisoner. Wouldn't he be proud!

And surprised. Nobody expects to catch a buzzard in a coon trap.

I slipped out of the shadows and made my way toward the door. I hadn't planned on striking up a conversation with Junior, but he spoke first.

"Oh, h-h-hi, d-d-doggie. My p-p-pa j-just went inside."

"I know, I saw the whole thing. Junior, I've always thought you were a pretty decent guy, but I'm afraid your old man is fixing to get busted."

"Oh d-d-darn. For w-w-what?"

"Stealing corn, wrecking sheds, you name it. We're going to throw the book at him."

I could see Junior, perched on the first big limb of a hackberry tree. He hung his head and gave it a sad shake. "P-p-p-poor old P-p-pa! Y-y-you w-w-won't h-hurt him, w-w-will you?"

"That's up to him. There's nothing personal in this, Junior. I'm just doing my job. Sorry."

I hurried on to the shed door, not wishing to see or hear any more of Junior's grief. I mean, it would be wrong to suppose that dogs in the Security Business don't have feelings. We do, and sometimes that makes it hard for us to do our jobs. Junior was a sweet guy, but his old man had turned to a life of crime, and now Junior was going to have to watch Wallace pay his debt to society.

I pushed these thoughts out of my mind and wiggled my way through the door. Inside, I gave my eyes a moment to adjust to the darkness, and suddenly it dawned on me that I hadn't heard the slam of the trapdoor. In other words, the pattern of clues was beginning to suggest that Wallace hadn't been caught.

I narrowed my eyes into Infrared Slits and did a slow scan of the shed. Sacks of feed, bales of hay . . . and the live-trap with the door still open. Oh brother, what a dunce! You know what he was doing? He was standing outside the trap, staring at the can of corn with big greedy eyes . . . and pecking at the criss cross of wire on the side of the trap!

I took a big breath of air, squared my enormous shoulders, and swaggered toward him. "Hank the Cowdog, Special Crimes. What's going on around here?"

Wallace whirled around at the sound of my voice. His ugly buzzard eyes grew wide and his beak fell open. "Well, what do you think's going

on here, dog? I'm trying to eat my dinner!"

"Oh? And what seems to be the problem?"

"Well, the problem is that I can see it but I can't reach it—as anyone with two eyes can see. Now, you just run along and leave me alone, hear?" He gave the wire five hard pecks and threw his wings into the air. "This is the most . . . I am fixing to lose my temper with this thing!" Again, he banged his beak against the wire, really whammed it, then rubbed his mouth. "Now, that hurt, that really hurt."

I tried my best not to laugh—I mean, this was a scream. *The buzzard was too dumb to walk into the trap!* I strolled over to him and looked into the cage.

"You know, pal, I just got here and maybe this sounds obvious, but there's some pretty stout wire between you and that can of corn."

He glared at me. "Dog, do I look dumb? Don't be nice, just tell the truth."

"Yes."

"Well, I ain't. It's very plain to me that there's some wire between me and that can of corn in yonder, and that's the whole problem. See, buzzards don't have any teeth. Did you know that?"

"I never thought about it."

"Well, think about it. If I had me a good set of

chainsaw teeth, I'd tear this thing to smithereens!"

"But you don't, right?"

He opened his mouth and pointed inside. "Look for yourself, pooch. Do you see any chain saws in there?"

"Nope."

He slammed his jaws shut. "Well, there you are. Don't go telling a buzzard how to run his business, unless you want to bite a hole in that wire yourself."

I had to chuckle. I mean, sometimes Security Work can be dull and depressing, but this was really funny. "Wallace, let's look at the problem from another angle. Suppose . . . just suppose there was a way of getting to that corn, without pecking a hole in the wire."

He stared at me. "Well, suppose that bird dogs could fly. Suppose that pigs rode side-saddles. Suppose my name was Lulu. Suppose don't mean a thing, puppy dog."

I laid a paw on his shoulder. "Wallace, look over there to the left and tell me what you see."

He squinted his eyes. "I see . . . some kind of door-outfit."

"A door! Is it open or closed?"

"It's . . . " He whipped his head around and beamed me a glare. "What are you trying to say?"

"Wallace, the door's wide open. All you have to do is walk in there and get your corn."

His eyes flicked back and forth, from me to the door and back to me. "That door ain't open."

"It is open."

"It ain't, 'cause if it was open, I would have seen it when I first walked in here."

"Wallace, the door is open, trust me."

He narrowed his eyes into cunning slits. "Okay, Mister Smartypants, if you think that door's open, which it ain't, then prove it."

I laughed in his face. "Okay, buddy, I'll prove it. Watch this and study your lessons." I strolled around to the front of the trap and stepped inside. "Now tell me, Wallace, was the door open or shut?"

He crossed his wings over his chest and turned his back on me. "I ain't talking."

"Am I inside the cage or outside?"

"Okay, maybe you're . . . dog, I don't know how you done that, but somehow you cheated. And just 'cause you're inside don't mean you can get to the corn, no it don't."

Again, I chuckled. "Wallace, you're something else. Watch and pay attention. I'll go through this once and then you can try it." I moved two steps to the west and placed a paw on the can of . . .

SLAM!

Huh?

I stared at Wallace and he stared at me. My mind was swirling, like leaves in a blizzard.

Wallace was the first to speak. "What was that?" He waddled over to the door and gave it a close inspection. "Well, glory be, the door slammed shut." Then his eyes popped open and an ugly grin spread across his beak. "Say, dog, this ain't a trap, is it?" I beamed him a glare of steel. He laughed. "Why, it *is* a trap, sure as shooting, and you was trying to . . . hee hee!"

At that very moment, Junior wiggled his head through the crack in the door. "P-p-pa, wh-what was that l-l-loud n-n-n-n-n . . . sound?"

Wallace clapped his wings together and cackled with glee. "You know, Junior, it's funny how things turn out. I think we've just trapped ourselves a dog!"

Oh, brother.

CHAPTER SEVEN

Wallace Sings a Dumb Little Song

I wish we could skip this part. You can't imagine how embarrassing it is. I mean, when the Head of Ranch Security finds himself . . . sigh. Well, let's mush on and get it over with.

Somehow I had managed to . . . I can't say it!

But I have to. By now you've figured it out yourself, so there's no use in trying to hide it.

Okay, the Road of Life has many twists and turns. Sometimes when we start out on a long journey, we don't always know, uh, where or how it will end. We all have plans, right? But sometimes those plans don't turn out right and then we experience the bitterness of . . . well, failure. We all feel the lash of failure once in a while—I mean it's normal and natural, and our ability to cope with failure is . . .

This is ridiculous. Hang on, here it comes, with no whipped cream. *I stepped into the trap and set off the trigger.* There! Now you know the awful truth.

It would have been bad enough if this had been my first Trap Experience. It wasn't. It was my second. It would have been bad enough if I'd been alone, but it was my incredible misfortune to be standing in front of an audience of buzzards.

Junior waddled into the shed, blinked his eyes, and flashed a silly grin. "Oh m-my g-g-goodness, a d-d-doggie in a t-t-trap, a trap!"

Wallace cackled with joy. "That's right, the dummy was a-trying to trap me and trapped hisself! Hee hee. Say, dog, could you pass me the corn? Hee hee!"

Between clenched teeth, I said, "Wallace, do me a favor. Get out of here and leave me alone. I need some quiet time."

"Heh, I bet you do. But you know what, pooch? All at once I'm feeling an urge to burst into song."

My heart sank. "Good grief!"

"You want to hear a song?"

"No."

"I ain't saying I'm a great singer, but do you want to hear my song?"

"No!"

He craned his neck in my direction and curled his beak. "Well, too bad, 'cause I'm fixing to sing one." He whirled around to Junior. "Son, give me a G." Junior hummed a note. Wallace shook his head. "That ain't a G, it's a G-whiz." Junior hummed another note and Wallace launched into one of the worst songs ever to disgrace this earth.

Don't Ever Step in a Trap

When I was a young guy and stood about
   knee-high
My daddy would tell me those tales
Of famous old buzzards who braved many
   hazards
When Texas was still up for sale.

They moved to the prairie when it wasn't very
Convenient for humans or pets.
And after each story, Pa told me some morey,
And here were the words that he said:

"Don't ever step in a trap, son,
Unless you're a dope or a sap, son.

Trapping's more fun when you ain't the one
Who's inside when the trigger goes SNAP!"

Old Daddy was shrewd, he knew what he knew,
Like most of them pioneering types.
They lived off the land, a man was a man.
They had to be tough to survive.

But manly and tough just wasn't enough,
They had to be cunning as well,
Catastrophes loomed and dummies were
    doomed,
And here's what my daddy would tell:

"Don't ever step in a trap, son,
Unless you're a dope or a sap, son.
Trapping's more fun when you ain't the one
Who's inside when the trigger goes SNAP!"

Now Daddy is gone. I'm trying to pass on
The wisdom I learned at his knee.
It's Junior who's young, and some would say
    dumb,
He's got a few bats in his tree.

So listen up, son, this life ain't all fun.
There's dangers and hazards and fate.

When you come to a trap, take a break, take
    a nap.
Let a chump go inside for the bait.

Don't ever step in a trap, son,
Unless you're a dope or a sap, son.
Trapping's more fun when you ain't the one
Who's inside when the trigger goes SNAP!

As you might expect, I had to listen to every
word of Wallace's pathetic little piece of musical
trash. I would have been happy to walk out after
the first line, but that wasn't an option. So I sat
there like a block of stone and beamed him a
murderous glare.

When he'd finished his assault on good taste
and music, Wallace took a bow and Junior
clapped his wings together. "Oh, that w-w-was g-
g-good, P-p-pa!"

"Thank you, thank you. Son, you might have
been crazy when you got here, but you're a-
talking sense now." He turned to me. "How 'bout
you, pooch? You ever heard finer music than
that?"

"Three stray cats with a bellyache couldn't
have sounded worse."

"Well now, I ain't ever claimed to be the best

singer in the world, but you've got to admit that it had a strong message."

Junior nodded. "Y-yeah, I l-l-learned a l-lot, P-pa."

Wallace grinned at me. "See? This younger generation ain't gone completely off the deep end. The song had a powerful message, puppy: traps are for dumbbells." He cackled. "And look where you're at! Hee hee."

His laughter echoed in my ears. "Are you through?"

"Well, maybe I am and maybe I ain't. If you gave me a few minutes, I might cobble up another tune. Would you like that?"

"No."

Wallace turned to Junior.

"He's kind of a sore loser, ain't he? And you know, I don't think he learned one thing from my song." Back to me. "Well, I can see that my talents ain't appreciated around here."

"That's for sure."

"So I reckon me and Junior'll just . . . " His eyes flashed and went to the can of corn. "Say there, neighbor, I don't suppose you'd mind passing that corn, would you? I mean, dogs don't eat corn and I hate to see good food go to waste."

An idea popped into my head. "Okay, sure.

Come closer and I'll see what I can do."

Heh heh. Have you figured out my wicked plan? Heh heh. Wallace was such a greedy-gut, he couldn't turn down a free meal.

He hopped over to the cage, licking his chops and rubbing his wings together. "Just hand it through a little at a time, pup."

I drew back a paw and gave the can a good slap. A moment later, Wallace was blinking his eyes, dripping juice off the end of his beak, and wearing most of the corn on his face. "Now, you didn't need to do that! Junior, did you see what he done?"

Now it was my turn to laugh. "That's what I think of you and your music, Wallace—corn for a corny song."

I thought that was a pretty good trick, but you know what? After he got over the shock, the old coot went right to work, pecking every corn kernel he could find. "It needs a little salt, but this ain't half-bad. Junior, you might want to get in on some of this."

Junior just grinned. "Oh, th-that's okay, P-p-pa. I'll just w-w-watch." He looked at me and shrugged. "H-h-he's kind of g-g-greedy, greedy."

"Yes, I noticed."

It took Wallace about a minute and a half to

clean up the corn. He flashed a smile, rubbed his belly, and burped. "Mighty fine, mighty fine. Corn's just corn, but it beats a poke in the eye." His gaze slid around to me. "And it beats sitting in a trap too. Hee hee! Boy, I know you're proud of yourself."

Junior shook his head. "P-p-pa, d-d-don't r-rub it in."

"Why not? Thunder, he tried to trap me in that thing!"

I said, "Yeah, but you were so dumb, you couldn't even find the door."

Wallace thought about that for a moment. "Well, it all worked out, didn't it? You're in the trap and I'm fixing to get airborne and hunt grub. Junior, let's move along. I've got a feeling there's a nice squashed rabbit a-waiting for me on the side of some lonely road."

Junior waved good-bye and slipped through the door. Wallace gave me one last wink and a sneer, and ducked outside. I heaved a sigh of relief. At last, peace and quiet!

I glanced around the shed, and suddenly the full weight of my dilemma came crashing down on my head. Holy smokes, how had I gotten myself into this mess? I mean, the whole idea of going inside the trap was to demonstrate . . . oh brother!

Slim would never understand this. When he showed up to check the trap, he would . . . gulp. I couldn't even imagine what he would say. I had to get out! I reached for the microphone of my mind and sent out an urgent APB.

"Hank to Drover, over. Attention please! This is Unit One. We need backup in the feed shed immediately! Repeat: We're calling for backup! This is not a drill, Drover, it's a Code Three Emergency! Do you copy?"

I strained my ears and listened. Nothing. No, wait! I seemed to be picking up a faint swishing noise, perhaps the sound of a small stub-tailed dog moving in my direction. I waited and hoped and listened to the pounding of my heart.

The sounds grew louder. Yes, it was Drover! He was coming to save me!

CHAPTER EIGHT

Ruined!

A moment later Drover wiggled through the crack in the door and popped inside. "Hank? Are you in here?"

"Drover, dearest pal, most trusted friend, I can't tell you how glad I am to see you!"

"Were you singing? I thought I heard someone singing."

"It was a couple of buzzards, but never mind. Gee, it's great to see you again. Come on in here. You look terrific."

"Thanks, me too." He gave me a peculiar look and cocked his head to the side. "Are you . . . did you get caught in the trap . . . again?"

"Drover, I know it looks that way, but . . . okay, yes, through a very strange chain of events, I did

71

in fact . . . that is, the trap caught me, yes. Would you like to hear the whole story?"

He yawned and sat down. "Oh, I guess so. Sure."

I told him the whole sad story. "So there you are. As you can see, I was just trying to do my job and no dog could have done more."

He nodded. "Yeah, but I guess you could have done less."

"What does that mean?"

"Well . . . maybe you shouldn't have gone inside the trap."

I glared at him through the wire. "Why are you repeating the obvious? Don't I know that? And Drover, it disturbs me that you seem to be grinning."

"Who, me?" He turned away so that I couldn't see his face, but I heard him snicker. "I guess the buzzards thought it was pretty funny."

"Oh sure, but what can you expect from a buzzard? They have no scruples, no sense of higher purpose. We dogs, on the other hand . . . Drover, you're not only grinning, but you're laughing."

"Not me. Hee huff muff ppfffft."

"Then why are you making those ridiculous sounds? Drover, I'm disappointed in you. This is an extremely serious situation and only a twisted mind would find humor in it."

"I know, but . . . honk snort . . . I can't help wondering what Slim's going to say when he . . . fffftttt."

The rest of his sentence disappeared into a fog of peculiar sounds. I wanted to blister him with angry words, but decided instead to, uh, try a softer approach.

"As a matter of fact, I've been thinking about that myself, and I think we can agree that this isn't going to look good. There's a high risk that Slim will view it as . . . well, as a sign of incompetence, and I don't need to remind you that it could smear the reputations of all of us in the Security Division."

"I know. Muff snort hee hee ppfffttt!"

"And that is no laughing matter." He muffed and honked and laughed some more. "But I can see that your heart has been corrupted, so let's go straight to the bottom line. Get me out of here!"

At last he managed to get control of himself. He throttled his laughter but he was still wearing a crazy grin that made me uneasy. "Well, I'd like to help, but I'm not good at opening doors."

"What's the big deal? It's got two latches, one at each side of the door, and all you have to do . . . look, Drover, this could ruin my career! Get over here and figure it out, and that is a direct order."

He wandered over to the trap and studied the latching mechanisms. He was still grinning. "Is that what the buzzards were singing about, you being caught in the trap?"

"Yes, as a matter of fact, it was, and would you mind concentrating on your business?"

"I'll bet it was a funny song."

"It was NOT a funny song. It was crude, rude, uncouth, noisy, and very disrespectful. Hurry up and get me out of here."

"What was the name of the song?"

I couldn't control the snarling muscles on my lips, and I showed him some serious fangs. "Do I care about the name of the song? No. I care about getting out of this incredible mess and saving my career. Hurry up!"

"Well, I'd kind of like to know the name of the song."

"Okay, that did it! You asked for this, buddy!" In a fit of righteous anger, I lunged at the runt and . . . BONK . . . more or less forgot about the wire, the very stout barrier of wire that . . . I rubbed my injured nose. "Let's see, you were asking about the title of a song?"

"Yeah, I'm kind of curious. I've never heard a buzzard sing."

"You've missed nothing, believe me, and I

74

must warn you that you'll be shocked and out-raged when you hear the name of the song."

"Oh gosh."

"He called it . . . something. 'Don't Ever Step in a Trap.' There. Are you shocked?"

His grin widened. "Not exactly. I think it's pretty cute."

"Drover, it's not cute and I'm deeply disap-pointed by your response, but we can talk about that later. Open the door."

"How did it go?"

"How did what go?"

"The song. Would you mind singing a little bit of it?"

I stared into the vacuum of his eyes. I couldn't believe this. "You think I'm going to . . . " I cut my eyes from side to side. I wasn't in a great bar-gaining position. "Drover, I'm glad that you're curious about these things, I mean, curiosity is a wonderful quality. If I sing you the chorus, will you promise to put this whole shabby incident behind us and concentrate on opening the door?"

"Oh sure, you bet."

"And I have your word on that?"

He raised his left paw in the air.

"Scout's Honor."

"You're not a Scout."

"Dog's Honor."

"Well, you're a dog, so that checks out." I heaved a sigh. "Here's the chorus." And with that, I sang him the tiresome thing:

Don't ever step in a trap, son,
Unless you're a dope or a sap, son.
'Cause trapping's more fun when you ain't
    the one
Who's inside when the trigger goes SNAP.

I studied his face, hoping to see . . . well, certain lines and wrinkles that might show anger and disgust and moral outrage. That's not what I saw. His silly grin grew even wider and he said . . . this is a direct quote . . . he said, "Oh, that's funny! Hee hee! That's hilarious! That's the funniest song I ever heard! What a great song!"

And then, before my very eyes . . . you won't believe this . . . the little dunce began staggering around, laughing his head off!

"Drover, this is disgraceful! Stop laughing and open this door! Soldier, I am giving you a direct order. Get me out of here immediately or I'll . . . Drover, you gave your Dog's Honor! Drover, come back here! Drover!"

I was stunned by this incredible turn of

events. I mean, not in my wildest dreams would I have supposed that the little slacker would stoop so low as to break his Solemn Oath of Dogness and leave me there, sitting in the ruins of my life. But that's exactly what he did.

His laughter faded into the distance and the silence rolled around me like . . . something. Like a wet cold blanket, like a funeral shroud. Gulp. Well, I'd really stepped in it this time and there wasn't a thing I could do about it. I didn't bother rehearsing a story for Slim. There would be no story.

For the next three hours, I sat in the trap, broiling over the fires of guilt and remorse. Those were the longest hours of my life. I couldn't even amuse myself by eating canned corn, since Wallace had hogged it all. I tried to pass the time with happy thoughts, but I could think of only one happy thought: if I ever got out of this mess alive, Drover would pay dearly for his treachery!

At last, streaks of light appeared through the cracks in the door. A shiver of dread passed through my body as I heard the sound of an approaching vehicle, its tires crunching the ground. I heard a door slam, then footsteps approaching. I swallowed hard and sat up straight. The door of the shed swung open, blinding me for a moment in the glare of sunbeams. Then I saw . . . Slim.

He stared at me. I said nothing, made no attempt to explain the unexplainable, and didn't even bother to tap my tail. His eyes rolled up inside his head and he slumped against the side of the shed.

I would have felt better if he'd screamed at me. Jumped up and down, stomped on his hat, pulled out some hair, foamed at the mouth, spit on the ground, bellowed, roared, yelled, fumed, called me ugly names. But no, all I received was his cold rebuking silence, and fellers, it cut me to the cricket.

He shook his head, blinked his eyes, and looked around. At last, he spoke. "How can I trap a coon when my dog keeps springing the trap?"

That was the burning question, all right, and I had no simple answers. Well, I had one simple answer: maybe I could stop walking into his idiot trap. But life is rarely so simple, and it certainly wasn't in this case. Slim knew nothing about the deeper aspects of the case, and he never would. How could I explain that I had been duped and tricked by a buzzard? There was no way of explaining it. The story was just too bizarre for wags, moans, and facial expressions.

I would go to my grave knowing the truth. Slim would go to his grave thinking that he had shared his life with a dumb dog. It couldn't be helped.

He came slouching toward the cage. I felt the cold glare of his eyes and couldn't look at him. I hung my head. He stood over me for a long time, saying nothing, then he spoke. "Well, did you enjoy the corn?"

No, I did NOT enjoy the corn. I didn't even get a bite of it. He didn't understand.

He opened the trapdoor and pointed a finger toward the rising sun. I took this to mean that I should leave the trap, leave the shed, and perhaps keep walking until I plunged off the face of the earth.

And that's what I did. With my tail trailing behind me like a piece of dead garden hose, I trudged outside, leaving behind a man who had once been my friend and a career that had once showed great promise.

I didn't go with Slim to feed cattle. Not only did he not want my company, but I didn't exactly crave his either. I wanted to be alone. I needed time to look over the pieces of my shattered life, to remember the good times and to cry over the tragedies.

And besides, I had already decided to keep walking. My career was finished and there was nothing to keep me on the ranch I had once served and loved. It broke my heart to think about it, but, yes, I would just keep walking until I turned into a skeleton and all my bones fell off and the buzzards came to pick them clean.

That was appropriate, don't you think? I would end my days as a snack for Wallace, and maybe he would sing another boring song over my bones.

I walked and walked and walked, until . . . well, I found myself standing in front of the machine shed. By then, I had grown a little weary and it occurred to me that it was a long way to the ends of the earth, and . . . well, I was hungry. Don't forget that I had spent the entire night . . . two entire nights cooped up in a coon cage.

I went to the overturned Ford hubcap that served as our dog bowl and began crunching tasteless kernels of Co-op dog food. Did I say *tasteless*? They weren't tasteless. They had the taste of stale grease and sawdust, but I didn't care, because that's just what I deserved—stale grease and sawdust.

Crunch, crunch.

When Wallace came to pick my bones, they

would taste like sawdust and grease, so that gave me one more cheerful thought. (My other cheerful thought was getting even with Drover.)

I was in the midst of brooding over my ruined life when I heard a vehicle approaching. I didn't bother to look around. I no longer cared. The vehicle stopped. A door opened and closed. Someone walked up behind me. Again, I didn't bother to look. I couldn't think of anyone I wanted to see . . . or anyone who might want to see me in this time of shame and disgrace.

"Hankie, do you feel pretty low?"

It was Slim's voice.

CHAPTER NINE

Buzzard Voodoo

I stopped chewing and looked up at him. Yes, I felt about as low as a dog could get without jumping into a well.

He knelt down beside me and I heard his knees pop. "Would a piece of my homemade beef jerky make you feel better?"

No. Yes. Maybe a little.

He brought a strip of jerky out of his pocket and held it under my nose. I sniffed it several times to make sure it wasn't his Gunpowder Recipe, the kind with enough hot pepper to melt your teeth. It wasn't, so I accepted his offering.

"You know, pooch, me and you are a lot alike."

Oh? I was sorry to hear that.

"We try to do good but we keep messing up.

But you know what? Having you around kind of gives me hope."

What did that mean?

"See, if you weren't here at the ranch, I might get to thinking that I'm the only one that makes bonehead mistakes."

Oh. Swell.

"So cheer up. I know you didn't mean to get caught in my trap two nights in a row. You're just a little light between the ears, is all."

Was this supposed to be making me feel better?

"But here's the deal, Hank." He aimed a finger at my nose. "Twice in a row is enough, and maybe you could find something else to do tonight, reckon? See, what I really want to catch is a coon."

Didn't I know that? Of course I knew it.

"Now, if you'll promise to be a good little doggie and stay out of my trap, we'll make up and be friends again."

Well . . .

"I know you've already busted that promise once, but this time maybe you can resist whatever temptation it is that makes you want to walk into a trap."

Temptation had nothing to do with it. I'd been trying to catch a buzzard and . . . I couldn't explain it.

He rubbed me behind the ears. "Let's go feed cows, and heck, maybe I'll even sing you a song."

Oh, please! What was the deal? All of a sudden, everybody on the ranch wanted to sing me a song!

He stood up and his knees popped again. "Let's go. It's a new day, and me and you are going to do our best not to mess it up."

Well . . . okay. If it would make him feel better, I would abandon my plans for walking to the ends of the earth and turning into a pile of bones. That had sounded like a lot of trouble anyway.

I followed him to the pickup. He opened the door and pointed inside. "I'll let you ride up front with the executives, if you promise not to throw up."

Could we skip the ancient history? For his information, I hadn't even seen a sprig of green grass, much less eaten one. And besides, I had learned my lesson.

I leaped up onto the pickup seat, went straight to the Shotgun Position, and off we went on a new feeding adventure. It wasn't all that exciting, but we got 'em fed. And Slim forgot about singing me a song, which came as a huge relief. I mean, we dogs try to be patient with our people, but honestly!

Oh, and Slim said no more about the Trap Debacle. For that, I was grateful. I thought he handled the situation pretty well, saying just enough to get his point across without being overbearing. We'd talked it over, dog to dog and man to man, and we'd reached a good understanding.

He wanted me to stay out of his raccoon trap and I had every intention of doing exactly that. I would never set foot inside the trap again. I would never get within ten feet of his stupid trap. Wild horses and camels couldn't drag me close to his stupid trap. And there the matter ended.

Forever. As darkness fell, I finished my evening walk-around of ranch headquarters and headed back to the office. You can guess who was already there, curled up on his gunnysack bed. Drover. I gave him a frigid glare and didn't speak. He sat up.

"Hi Hank. I guess you're mad at me."

"No. 'Mad' is a three-letter word and it doesn't begin to cover what I feel."

"So . . . pretty mad, huh?"

"What do you think? You little traitor! You left me in the trap and that's where Slim found me this morning. How do you suppose that made me feel?"

"Did you get fired?"

"No, I didn't get fired, Drover, I quit. I quit in

disgrace, but Slim begged me to come back."

He leaped to his feet and started wig-wagging his stub tail. "Oh goodie, I'm so glad!"

"Well, you won't be glad for long. On your feet, soldier."

"I already am."

"Don't argue with me. March to the nearest corner and put your nose in it."

"Oh drat."

"March!"

Drover whined and moaned, but I didn't care. He straggled over to the nearest angle-iron leg of the gas-tank platform and put his nose against it. He let out a moan. "I hate sticking my nose in the corner!"

"Good. Great. Tell me how much you hate it."

"Well . . . I hate it more than dirt."

"Keep going."

"I hate it more than water."

"I love it. Keep talking."

"I hate it more than sneezing."

I feasted my eyes on his misery. "So the point is that you wish you were somewhere else, right?"

"Yeah, almost anywhere."

"Now you know how I felt inside that trap. Are you sorry you walked away and left me there to rot?"

"I knew you wouldn't rot."

"Drover, are you sorry or not?"

"Yeah, but . . . I couldn't help myself. I couldn't stop laughing."

I looked away and heaved a sigh. "See, that's the part that hurts me the most. I was alone, helpless, and miserable, and you thought it was funny! What kind of dog are you?"

He was almost in tears. "It was the song that did it. I think it was some kind of . . . voodoo song."

I studied the mutt for a moment. "Voodoo song? What do you mean?"

"Well, it made me act crazy. I wanted to help, but that song just . . . oh, I feel awful!"

I began pacing, as I often do when a light begins to shine at the end of the turnip. "Let me get this straight. You're saying that the words of the song penetrated your mental mind and took control of your body?"

"Yeah, that's just what happened. It was really spooky."

"Hmmm. This is interesting, Drover, and I must admit that it's an angle I hadn't considered. That song was written and performed by a buzzard, you know."

"I know."

"I know you know. That's what I just said, and

don't interrupt me." I continued pacing. "Buzzards look kind of spooky, don't they?"

"Yeah, they're so ugly, they give me the creeps."

"And there's a connection between creepy and voodoo, right? Of course, why didn't I think of this sooner!" I whirled around and faced him. "I've got it worked out, son. Don't you get it? That song put some kind of spell on you."

"Gosh, I never thought of that. You mean . . . "

"Yes! Wallace knew exactly what he was doing. He vexed you with voodoo!"

"You mean hexed?"

"You never would have laughed at my misfortune if you hadn't been under some kind of wicked spell."

"Oh goodie. Can I take my nose out of the corner?"

"Not yet." I resumed pacing. "Oh, they're clever, these villains. But who would have suspected a buzzard? Not you, obviously, but what really scares me is that I fell for it too, like a lamb to the slobber."

"Slaughter."

"What?"

"Like a lamb to the slaughter. You said slobber."

I curled my lip at him. "Do you want to correct my spelling or hear the rest of my report?"

"My neck's getting tired."

"I don't care. Pay attention." I paced away from him again, my mind racing. "Wallace had the whole thing planned from the start and you walked right into his trap."

"No, I think it was you."

"I walked into the *actual* trap, but you walked into the unactual trap. In other words, Drover, we were both trapped by the same villain. We were helpless victims of a conspiracy."

"Gosh, you mean . . . "

I marched over to him. "Yes. This court finds you innocent of all charges."

"That's weird."

"You're out of jail and free to go."

"Oh boy!" He removed his nose from the corner and grinned. Then his grin faded. "Yeah, but I don't know where to go."

"Well, go to your room."

"I'm already in my room."

I whopped him on the back with my paw. "You see? Everything has worked out for the best. Let's hit the sacks." We went straight to our respective gunnysacks and flopped down. After a moment of silence, I said, "Drover, I'm sorry I got mad at you."

"Oh, that's okay."

"I thought you were just being a chicken liver and a weenie."

"Yeah, I'm starved."

"It never occurred to me that you were under the spell of Buzzard Voodoo."

"I love chicken liver."

"In a moment of weakness and despair, I blamed you, Drover, and I'm deeply sorry. Can you ever forgive me?"

"Boy, that was a funny song. Hee hee."

I stared at the outline of his face. "What?"

"I said . . . it's not funny when you're wrong."

"Oh. Good point." I took a deep breath of air. "Well, Drover, I'm glad we were able to work through this crisis. Lights out. Let's grab some sleep. This whole nasty episode is behind us forever."

I thought it was over forever, but at that very moment I heard a sound that sent the case plunging into a new and dangerous direction. You'll never guess what it was.

CHAPTER TEN

Drover Disappears in the Night

Okay, let me reset the skinerio. If you recall, Drover and I had just finished a heart-to-heart talk, a very moving discussion about our personal problems. Drover had admitted . . . I had admitted . . . it was kind of complicated, so we'll skip the details.

The point is that Drover had won his release from prison and we had saved our friendship from the wicked plot of Wallace the buzzard.

In other words, the cause of Justice had been served on a plate of finest china, and we were feasting on . . . something. We were sharing a moment of peace and tranquittery. But then . . .

I heard a sound, a kind of snapping sound. Drover heard it too. We lifted our heads and found ourselves staring into each other's eyes. I was the first to speak.

"What was that?" Drover rolled his eyes around.

"I don't know. I think it came from . . . the feed shed."

"The feed shed? Hmm, I wonder . . . the feed shed!"

"Oh my gosh, do you reckon it could be . . . the trap?"

I sprang to my feet and tried to clear the fog out of my bog . . . the fog out of my head. "Feed shed . . . trap. I feel there's a connection here, Drover. There's a coon trap in the feed shed, remember?"

"Yeah, that's what we were just talking about."

My eyes probed the darkness as the clues began knitting themselves into a pattern. "You're right. We've caught something! But you've ignored a very important detail. This time it's not ME in the trap."

"I'll be derned."

"Which is the best news of the year. Do you see the meaning of this?"

"Well, let me think."

"We've caught the thief, Drover, the same thieving buzzard who caused us so much grief."

"Oh boy!"

"And I've got even better news, son. We're

going to send a scouting party down to the shed."

"That'll be fun."

"And I'm appointing *you* to the job."

He stared at me for a moment, then rose to his feet and began limping around in a circle. "You know, I'd love to go, but all at once this old leg . . . "

"I don't want to hear about your 'old leg.' I promised Slim that I would never go near that trap again, and I won't."

"Yeah, but . . . oh, my leg!"

"Soldier, you've gotten your orders, and you *will* carry them out."

"You mean . . . "

"Yes." I stuck my nose in his face and showed him some fangs. "If you try to slip off to the machine shed, like you've done so many times before, I will personally see that you're barbecued over an open fire."

"Yeah, but . . . "

"Go! I'll be waiting right here for your report." He moaned and whimpered, but I showed him mo nursery. No mercy. "And don't let Wallace sing you any songs. Don't forget, he pulls sneaky tricks."

I watched until he disappeared into the darkness. Oh, and I noticed a very interesting detail. He limped and dragged himself along for the first fifty feet, then his limp vanished. Does that sound suspicious? I thought so.

See, for years I'd been gathering information on Drover's so-called limp, and the file had grown as thick as a Dallas phone book. We still didn't have enough evidence to bring formal charges against the runt, but it was beginning to appear that he was *faking that limp*.

Are you shocked? I know, it's hard to believe that a member of the Elite Guards would stoop to such shabby behavior, but there you are. I would add this latest information to his file.

Well, it appeared that everything was working out, and my spirits were soaring. If Drover returned with a good report, the ranch would be rid of a nuisance. Come morning, Slim would find a buzzard in the trap, instead of me, and he would be very proud that I had honored my solemn oath to stay away from the trap. Life on the ranch would return to normal, and we would liverly happy afterly.

We would live happily ever liverwurst.

We would live . . . phooey.

Anyway, I was in a great mood. I set the stop-watch of my mind and began counting time. I calculated that Drover should be returning in . . . oh, five minutes. Six minutes. Ten minutes. With

Drover, we have to add a little time for him to dawdle along, stare at the moon, and chase crickets.

An hour later, I began to worry. After two hours, I had paced a road through the middle of the office. Where was he! Maybe something bad had happened: he'd been voodooed by a buzzard, mugged on his way home, kidnapped by coyotes, lost his way, wandered off into the pasture . . .

With Drover, the list of possible disasters was endless.

All my natural instincts told me to go looking for the little mutt, but what if I did, and ended up going into the feed shed? That was something I had pledged not to do, and, well, a pledge is a pledge. But if anything happened to the little guy, I would never forgive myself.

This had become one of the heaviest moral decisions of my whole career, and it seemed a perfect time to . . . well, sing a song about the kind of heavy moral decisions that dogs have to face at the top of Life's Mountain. Here, listen to this.

The Heavy Moral Decision Song

My solemnest oath I offered to Slim,
My cowboy companion and loyalest friend.

My honor demands that I'm loyal to him.
I'd never go back on my oath on a whim.

Temptation can act as a type of a wedge
That's driven by somebody swinging a sledge,
Dividing the mind and pushing the edge.
But fellers, a pledge is a pledge is a pledge!

But here's the dilemma: I'm fearing the worst.
Poor Drover is lost and this isn't the first
Occasion when he's been so deeply immersed
In trouble, he needed the use of a hearse.

I'm deeply divided here, pulled half in two.
This moral decision has left me to stew.
My friendship to both of them's always been
    true.
So what in the heck is a dog s'posed to do?

But wait, there's a voice inside of my head
That's urging alternative action instead.
I heard it real plain and here's what it said:
"Hankie, forget it and go back to bed."

What did you think of the song? Okay, maybe
it wasn't all that great, but I came up with it on
short notice. And it beat anything a buzzard

could have written. Anyway, it gives you some idea of the kind of wrenching decisions the Head of Ranch Security faces every day of the year.

And it also gave you my solution. Heh heh. Go back to bed. Forget about the whole mess.

Why not? I mean, just because we face heavy decisions doesn't mean we have to come up with answers. Who's running this ranch, me or the heavy decisions? I'm running the ranch and if I want to take a vacation and become an irresponsible toad, that's exactly what I'll do.

And that's what I did. I turned off the lights, crawled underneath my gunnysack bed, pulled the covers over my eyes and ears, and ceased thinking about anything that involved Slim or Drover.

By George, they had their lives and I had mine.

It worked. Okay, it worked for about three minutes and then . . . sigh . . . I couldn't stand it any longer. I know what you're thinking. I'd gotten too deeply involved in this case, I deserved a night off . . . yeah, yeah, yeah. I had the same thoughts, but they didn't do any good. Duty was calling and Drover needed help.

I rose to my feet and took a big gulp of air. I really didn't want to do this. I'm not inclined to be superstitious, but I must admit that I had bad feelings about going back toward the feed shed and putting myself anywhere close to that trap. A trap's just a trap, you might argue, something made of steel and wire, but I had a history of lousy luck with that particular trap. Why, if something went wrong and I got myself sucked into that thing a third time . . .

A cold shiver passed through my entire body. I didn't even want to think about it. Slim was a good man, but if I ended up inside that trap a third night in a row . . . ooo boy, we didn't need to walk through that graveyard. I would have to make sure it didn't happen.

I left the office and took the elevator down to the first floor. There, I picked up Drover's scent and followed it in a westerly direction. I kept hoping that I would pick up a second trail, indicating that the little goof had checked the trap, left the shed, and wandered off into the pasture.

No such luck. The trail led straight to the feed shed, and there was no indication that he had come back outside.

At that point, a new idea began to glow in the back of my mind. Gee, what if the sound we'd heard *hadn't* been the trapdoor. What if Drover had bungled into the trap and set off the trigger . . . and trapped himself! It could have happened while I was doing my song, right? The door could have

slammed shut and I never would have heard it.

This would be a great tragedy, of course. Hee hee. I'm sorry, I didn't mean to laugh. It would be a tragedy and another blow to the reputation of the Security Division, but on the other hand . . . hee hee . . . Drover had thought it was pretty funny that I'd gotten trapped, so by George, if he was inside the trap, I saw nothing wrong with laughing my head off.

Maybe you think it wasn't nice of me to have such wicked thoughts, but don't forget that sharing is very important, and that includes sharing blame and shame. I wanted to share the experience with Drover, that's all.

I crept up to the feed-shed door and listened. I could hear . . . something, a swishing sound and then a voice. I couldn't make out any words, but it was Drover's voice.

Hmmm. Obviously he wasn't in any danger and that came as a relief, and I was now more convinced than ever that . . . hee hee . . . he'd got caught in the trap. All the clues pointed in that direction. See, if we'd caught a buzzard, Drover wouldn't have hung around in the shed. I mean, he was scared of Buzzard Voodoo and he would have streaked back to the office to give me the news.

That made perfect sense. No, he was inside

the trap, talking to himself. I could hardly conceal my delight. My concern, that is. Smiling to myself, I dropped down on my belly and wiggled myself through the crack in the door. "Well, Drover, how does it feel to . . . "

HUH?

CHAPTER ELEVEN

Eddy's Phony Helicopter

Stand by for some shocking news. Remember all those clues that proved without a doubt that Drover had gotten trapped? Forget the clues. Sometimes clues take us in the right direction and sometimes they don't. This time, the clues had given us some very misleading information.

When I wiggled myself inside the shed, I was shocked and astounded to see that Drover was not inside the trap, muttering to himself. You know who was inside the trap? Not Wallace, as you might have thought, but . . . Eddy the Rac!

Yes, my old buddy was still following a life of crime, and this time he'd gotten himself caught. Oh, sweet Justice!

So far, so good. But the weird part was that

Drover had remained in the shed. Why hadn't he brought me the news? It didn't make sense.

My sudden appearance startled them, and Drover gave me a guilty smile. "Oh hi. We caught Eddy and I was just coming to tell you."

I lumbered over to him and gave him a scorching glare. "You were coming to tell me? Drover, you've been in here for two hours. I was worried sick. I couldn't imagine what had become of you, and I still can't."

"Well, I was just . . . Eddy was showing me some magic tricks."

"Magic tricks?"

My steely gaze moved from Drover to Eddy. There he sat in the middle of the cage, the same little crook I'd known before, only older and a little bigger. *A little bigger?* That doesn't sound right, does it? I mean, he was either bigger or littler, but he couldn't have been both, so let's change that to, "He looked somewhat bigger."

But he was the same guy who'd once been Slim's pet. I could have picked him out of any police lineup.

A stranger seeing Eddy might have said, "Oh, what a cute little raccoon! Isn't he darling?" See, coons have certain qualities that cause humans and even a few dogs to notice their "cuteness."

They have that black mask over their eyes, they walk like a bear, and they have five-fingered hands that look very much like human hands.

If you've never had dealings with raccoons, you might call them "cute" and laugh at the funny things they do. But I'd had plenty of dealings with coons and I knew they weren't so cute. Those little hands, for example, were always moving around, and they had a way of finding mischief. With those hands, they could pull garbage out of a barrel, steal eggs out of a chicken nest, rip open feed sacks, wreck barns, open doors, and escape from almost any kind of enclosure.

At the moment, Eddy's hands weren't involved in mischief, but they were busy nonetheless. He was rolling an empty corn can around in his hands and pitching it up into the air.

He saw me glaring at him and in his squeaky little voice, he said, "Oh, hi. How's it going?"

I pushed my way past Drover and moved closer to the trap. "Hello, Eddy. Remember me?"

"Sure. You bet. Guard dog, right? Bark, stuff like that?"

"That's partly correct. I'm Head of Ranch Security and sometimes I bark, but I have other jobs that are even more important. I conduct investigations, solve crimes, and arrest foolish raccoons who walk into my traps."

"Right. Want to see a trick?"

Before I could answer, Drover said, "You've got to see this, Hank, it's really neat."

"Drover, it's time for you to buzz off. I have to wring a confession out the prisoner and it won't be pretty."

"Yeah, but he can make that can disappear."

I stuck my nose in his face. "What part of 'buzz off' don't you understand? I have to interrogate the prisoner and I can't concentrate with you jabbering about magic tricks. Go back to the office and wait for further orders. Good-bye."

Drover hung his head and started toward the door. "Well, gosh, you don't need to talk so mean. We were just having a little fun."

"Yes, I noticed. For two solid hours, you were goofing off and having fun with a notorious crinimal. That's against regulations and it will show up in my report. Now scram!"

He wiggled out the door and I turned back to the prisoner. "Okay, Eddy, let's get this over with."

"Nice little guy."

"What?"

"Rover. Nice little guy."

"His name's Drover, with a *d*, and he's a nice little moron. Sometimes I wonder why I keep him on the payroll."

"He liked my tricks."

"Yeah, well, morons are easily entertained. The bad news is that I don't have the slightest interest in your tricks."

"They're cool."

"I don't care." I found myself looking at him through the wire. "Eddy, how did you get yourself into this mess? I mean, you had the whole Texas Panhandle as your playground, but you came back to my ranch and got yourself trapped."

He rolled his eyes around. "Wanted some corn. Hungry."

"Eddy, the creek is full of fish and frogs and other things that coons are supposed to eat. You didn't need to start stealing corn and wrecking sheds."

His eyes roamed the cage. "Bored. Moonlight Madness. Moon comes up, I've got to boogie."

Yes, I knew all about Moonlight Madness—Eddy's excuse for getting into mischief. "Right, and look what it got you."

"Got to get out! Hole, got to find a hole." He moved a full circle around the cage, testing the wire with his hands. "Here? No. Here? No. Where's the hole?" He seized the wire with both hands and gave me a pleading look. "You can help. The door."

"Eddy, Eddy! You know I can't do that. We're on opposite sides of the law."

"Just for old times? Please?"

I shook my head and began pacing in front of the cage. "I hate this, Eddy. It gives me no pleasure to see you behind bars, but you broke the law. You have no . . . "

"Self-discipline?"

"Exactly. You have no self-discipline. You're a slave to your . . . "

"Impulses?"

"Right, but if you don't mind, I'll do the talking."

"Sure. No problem."

"The sad fact, Eddy, is that you're just a little crook. Sometimes you're a nice little crook, but in my business a crook is still a crook."

"Ever ride in a helicopter?"

I stopped in my tracks. "What?"

"Helicopter. Ever ride in one?"

"No."

"Ever want to?"

"Sure, who hasn't? Why do you ask?"

"Just curious."

I resumed my pacing. "Well, you've never been short of curiosity, pal, and that's part of your problem. See, curiosity is good up to a point, but then it starts getting nosy little raccoons into . . . "

Just then, I noticed that he was doing something unusual inside the cage. He was sitting near the front of the cage and . . . I looked closer. Was he speaking into the empty corn can? Yes, almost as though he were . . . well, talking into a microphone.

"Tower? Eddy One. Over."

I moved closer to the cage. "What are you doing now?"

He held up a finger to his lips. "Shhh. Talking to the tower."

I glanced around the shed. "The tower? What tower?"

Again, he spoke into the can. "Tower? Eddy One. Permission to start engine. Over." Then he held the can up to his left ear and listened. He nodded and moved the can back to his mouth. "Roger that. Thanks." He turned to me. "Better stand back."

This was making no sense to me and I had no intention of standing back, but then I heard this odd sound: THOCK, THOCK, THOCK. And all at once, I felt it might be a good idea to . . . well, step back.

I moved away from the cage and listened as

the "thock-thock-thock" changed into a steady roar. Inside the cage, Eddy's hands moved around in front of him, almost as though he were . . . well, flipping switches or something.

What was the deal? Coons didn't make sounds like that, did they? I mean, I knew they could click, chirp, growl, croon, and make other kinds of noises, but what I'd heard sounded a whole lot like . . . well, some kind of motor or machine.

A helicopter.

"Hey Eddy, I can see you're busy doing something, but I was wondering . . . "

He held up a paw for silence and spoke into the . . . whatever it was, the can or the microphone. "Tower? Eddy One. Ignition. Good to go." He turned back to me. "What?"

"What's all the noise about, and who's this so-called tower you're talking to?"

He heaved a sigh and shook his head. "Control tower. Helicopter. Test flight."

I stared into his beady little eyes and burst out laughing. "Helicopter! Control tower! Are you crazy?"

"Just a little spin." He held his clenched hands out in front of him, as though he were gripping steering levers or something, and . . . gee, the roar of the engine grew louder.

Over the roar, I yelled, "Hey Eddy, there must be some mistake. That's a cage, not a helicopter."

He gave me an impatient scowl. "Things change. Constant flux. Thermodoodle dynamics. Energy shift. Quantum combobulations. You didn't know?"

"I didn't say I didn't know. It just sounds crazy, that's all."

He shrugged. "You want to go for a spin?"

"Ha ha ha. Me, go for a spin in a cage that you say is a helicopter? Ha ha."

"Might as well. Short ride. Great experience."

"Absolutely not."

He shrugged. "Fine. Stay here." Again, he spoke into the microphone . . . the empty corn can. I refused to believe he was talking into a microphone. "Tower? Eddy One. Permission to lift off. Over." He looked at me. "Better stand back. I'm cleared."

I blinked my eyes in wonder. "Hey, hold on a second, don't leave yet." I went to the door of the shed and peered outside, just to be sure Drover wasn't spying on me. He was nowhere in sight, so I went back to Eddy and his . . . whatever it was. His phony helicopter.

Eddy and I were fixing to have a serious talk about this business.

Eddy Walks into My Trap

I marched up to the cage and gave Eddy a stern glare, the kind of stern glare an officer of the law gives to raccoons who think they're flying helicopters. "Eddy, I've got several problems with this. Turn off the engine."

He flicked a switch and . . . well, the motor died. Again, he seemed impatient. "Okay, shoot. Hurry."

"Don't tell me to hurry, and don't forget who's in charge around here. Number one, it's hard for me to forget that you have a history of being a sneak. I don't mean to sound rude, but Eddy, you've pulled tricks on me before. This could be another of your famous tricks."

He shrugged. "I was young, foolish. I'm a pilot now. Can't mess around."

I searched his face, looking for the tiny clues that might indicate that he was telling me a gigantic whopperous lie. After you've been in the Security Business a few years and had dealings with the crinimal element, you develop certain skills for smoking out the ones who don't tell the truth. I'm sorry, but we don't have time to go into any details on Whopper Detection.

Or do we? I guess it wouldn't hurt.

Okay, let's start with Shifty Eyes. Your crooks and your crinimal types almost always have shifty eyes. When they tell a whopper, their eyes tend to drift around and they won't make eye contact. If you're trained in Whopper Detection Techniques, you can pick up the signals right away.

After the eyes, we check out the Body Lingo. These are tiny details that would escape the notice of an unobserved trainer . . . an untrained observer, shall we say: sagging shoulders, rapid breathing, a line of perspiration on the upper lip, sweaty palms, sagging shoulders, rapid breathing, and sweaty palms.

That's a long list, isn't it? Dogs with no training would miss all the tiny details or wouldn't bother to look for them. In our department, we take the time and we notice. As a result, we have one of the highest rates of Whopper Detection in the entire state of Texas.

I don't mean to brag, but facts are facts. Who else is going to tell you these things? Anyway, that gives you a little glimpse at the secret techniques we use in our work.

Eddy had no idea that he was being watched, observed, measured, and analyzed by a highly trained professional. I mean, what does a raccoon know about anything? They know a lot about making mischief and wrecking things, but they lack the kind of deeper intelligence that might allow them to understand Whopper Detection.

It's been said that coons are smart. Ha. Ask an expert about coons. Ask me, for example, and I'll tell you that they're smart enough to get into trouble but not smart enough to get out of it. I mean, look who was in the trap.

Okay, maybe I'd been in that same trap a few times myself, but that had been under very different circumstances. I'm sure you'll agree that it doesn't apply to this situation, so let's mush on with the investigation.

There was Eddy inside the trap, and there I was outside the trap, probing and studying and analyzing his every move and gesture. His gaze wandered around, then landed on me. "Want to see a trick?"

"No. I'm busy."

"Boring." He started juggling the empty corn can, pitching it from one hand to the other. Then, all at once and before my very eyes, the can just . . . well, disappeared. I narrowed my eyes and took a closer look.

"Hey, where'd the can go?"

He giggled. "Gone. Poof. Thin air. Hee hee."

My probing gaze swept the cage. No can. "Eddy, you're still my prisoner and I said no tricks. Where's the can?"

Eddy's eyes darted around. He looked under one armpit and then the other. He grinned and shrugged his shoulders. "Disappeared."

"Eddy, cans don't disappear and I don't believe in magic. Where's the can?"

He gave me a look of perfect innocence (that made me nervous) and stood up. Huh? I'll be derned. He'd been sitting on the corn can.

He grinned and started rolling his fingers. "No problem. Now you see it, now you don't. Hee hee. Want another trick?"

"No, I don't want another trick. Sit down and behave yourself. For your information, I'm conducting a Whopper Detection Test and you're making it very difficult."

"Yeah? Whoppers? Maybe I can help."

I laughed in his face. "Ha ha ha. Oh, that's rich, Eddy. I'm out here running diagnostics to determine if you're telling me outrageous lies, and you're offering to *help*? Ha ha! You're the champ, pal, I'll give you that." The laughter died in my throat. I glanced over both shoulders and moved closer to him. "What do you mean, help?"

He threw out his open hands, palms up. "See? Dry palms."

I narrowed my eyes at his alleged palms. They seemed to be . . . uh . . . dry. "Okay, dry palms and so what?"

He pointed to his upper lip. "You see any sweat?"

"No, I don't see any sweat. What's your point?"

He stared directly into my eyes. "Eye contact. What do you think?"

Our gazes locked for a long moment. "I'll tell you what I think, you little swindler. You got into our Document Vault and read our secret manuals on Whopper Detection, that's what I think. I don't know how you did it, but you're giving me the creeps. I'm leaving. Good-bye."

I marched toward the shed door. Behind me,

he said, "How come you don't believe in helicopters?"

I stopped in my tracks and looked back at him. "Eddy, I believe in helicopters. I just don't believe . . . I refuse to believe that you're sitting in one, or that you could fly it if it really were a helicopter, which it isn't."

"How'd I do on the Whopper Test?"

In the long silence, I searched for an answer. "You passed. And you know what?" I paced back to the cage. "That really shakes me to the boots of my foundations. I know you, Eddy. I know all your patterns and tendencies, and telling the truth isn't even on your chart."

He studied the ceiling for a moment. "You'll never know. Unless you go for a ride."

I put my nose against the wire. "Eddy, I will not go for a ride. I will never go for a helicopter ride in a coon trap. Am I making myself clear?"

"Short spin. Five minutes."

"No."

"Four minutes."

"No!"

"Okay, two. Two minutes. Then you'll know."

My mind tumbled. I was absolutely sure that this was just another of his con games, but on the other hand . . . I trotted back to the shed door and peered outside. Nobody was spying, so I made my way back to the trap.

"Okay, pal, two minutes, but that's it."

He clapped his hands together and gave me an admiring look. "You're brave. Real courage."

"Shut up, Eddy. The more you talk, the more I worry. How do I get into your so-called helicopter? Can two of us fit into the cockpit?"

He squeaked a laugh. "Sure. Easy." He scampered over to the cage door and reached a hand through the wire, so that he was touching one of the two latches. "I'll push this one. You push that one with . . . "

"Don't tell me what to do. I'm still in charge here."

"Right. Sorry."

I swaggered over to the trapdoor and studied the latching mechanism. "Okay, you push down on that latch over there and I'll press on this one."

"Great idea. Never thought of that."

"When both latches are free, you raise the door and hold it open. Got it?"

"Got it."

"While the door is open, I'll scoot into the copilot seat. Got that?"

"Roger, Captain!"

Captain. You know, I liked the sounds of that. It showed some respect. I mean, Eddy was a hardhead, but I guess he'd finally figured out who was boss around here. Heh heh. Me. The Captain.

The door-opening maneuver went off without a hitch, I mean, just as though we'd been practicing it for weeks. This served as further proof that when Eddy put his mind to it, he could be a pretty good member of the team.

See, at some point in the last five minutes, Eddy and I had ceased being old rivals. We had put our minds and talents together and had forged ourselves into a team of pilots who were fixing to take this aircraft out on its first solo flight. It would be dangerous mission. I knew it, Eddy knew it, but we were willing to risk our very lives to further the cause of Knowledge and Science.

And we would do it as a Team.

To tell you the truth, it was a pretty emotional moment for both of us. After weeks and months of training . . . reading manuals, learning the instrumentation, logging hours in the flight stimulator, going over every inch of the ship . . . after all the training and so forth, we were finally ready to knock a hole in the sky and soar like birds.

You know, I'd always dreamed of flying a helicopter.

I waited until I heard the hatch close, then I gave Eddy a little surprise. "Oh, there's been a change in plans. I'm going to fly the ship myself. You're copilot."

He stared at me through the wire. "Really?"

"Eddy, you're pretty good with your hands, but for this mission, we need nerves of steel and, well, the kind of broad experience I bring to the team."

He heaved a sigh. "Darn."

"I'm sorry, but I have to pull rank. Are we ready?"

"You go without me."

I laughed. "No, you don't understand. See, it'll take both of us to fly this thing because . . . "

HUH?

I stared at the wire. It appeared that . . . uh . . . I was inside the wire enclosure and Eddy was . . . I cut my eyes from side to side.

"Eddy, disregard what I just said. It was a joke. You take the controls." He monkey-walked over to a sack of feed and ripped a hole in it. "Eddy, this is no time for you to be thinking of food."

He raked some feed cubes out of the sack,

picked through them with his busy little hands, and held one up. He crunched the end off it. "Want a bite?"

I glared at him through the wire. "No, I do not want a bite! Get in here and fly the ship! That is a direct order!" He went on eating. I was beginning to feel uneasy about this. "Eddy, I must ask you an urgent question, and I want the truth." I took a gulp of air. "Eddy, is this thing really a helicopter?"

He took his sweet time in answering, gobbled down the rest of the feed cube, and nibbled the crumbs off his fingers. Then he looked me straight in the eyes and said, "Nope. Coon trap. Hee hee. I'm a rat. They ought to lock me up."

And then he proceeded to rip open three more sacks and scattered feed cubes from one end of the shed to the other.

"Okay, pal, that's it. You're under arrest! Eddy?"

Oh brother!

Well, I guess you can imagine the rest of the story. At eight o'clock the next morning, Slim arrived. He stepped into the shed and . . . we don't need to go into all the details. It wasn't pleasant or funny.

But before you burst into tears, let me tell you a little secret. It didn't turn out as badly as you might think. See, after a coon wrecks a place and eats his weight in thirty-eight percent protein range cubes, what do you suppose he does? He finds a comfortable spot, curls up in a ball, and goes to sleep. And that's exactly what the little mutter-mumble did.

I'll be the first to admit that it looked pretty bad, him sleeping on top of a trap that held the Head of Ranch Security, but the important thing is . . .

See, I had known all along that if I played along with Eddy's scam and stalled for time, he would . . . he would eventually fall asleep. No kidding. It's typical coon behavior. And, hey, he walked right into my . . . uh . . . trap, so to speak. Honest.

When Slim walked in, Eddy was zonked, out cold, sleeping as only a coon can sleep after a long night of Moonlight Madness. All Slim had to do was pick him up by the scruff of his neck, haul him two miles to another part of the ranch, and leave him sleeping in the fork of a cottonwood tree.

Hencely, through stealth and cunning, I had managed to break the case wide open and rid the ranch of a crafty little feed burglar. Pretty amazing, huh? You bet.

ZZZZZ

Now tell the truth, did you think I was the one who got scammed? Did you think that I actually fell for that . . . for that ridiculous story about the helicopter? Ha ha. Not me, fellers, I was on top of the case from start to finish. No kidding.

Of course Slim never figured it out. He groaned and fumed and called me hateful names, and then he and Loper laughed about it for a solid week—"old Birdbrain" getting caught in the coon trap three nights in a row.

It was shameful. I mean, what more did they want? I'd caught the crook and solved the case. Oh well. As long as you and I know the truth, that's all that matters.

The Case of the Tricky Trap is closed.

Honest, I never believed that story about the helicopter. Who would believe such baloney? Not me.

The following activities are samples from *The Hank Times*, the official newspaper of Hank's Security Force. Do not write on these pages unless this is your book. Even then, why not just find a scrap of paper?

"Photogenic" Memory Quiz

We all know that Hank has a "photogenic" memory—being aware of your surroundings is an important quality for a Head of Ranch Security. Now you can test your powers of observation.

How good is your memory? Look at the illustration on page 16 and try to remember as many things about it as possible. Then turn back to this page and see how many questions you can answer.

1. Was Hank's tongue pointing to the left or the right?

2. Could you see the license plate on the front bumper?

3. Was Drover looking to HIS left or right?

4. Were there 0, 1, or 2 windshield wipers?

5. Could you see more fingers on Slim's fingers left hand or his right hand?

6. How many of Hank's eyes were looking up: 0, 1, 2 or, 3?

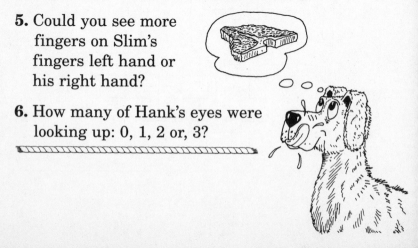

Drover's Dilemma

Help Drover find his way out of the oval below.

Eye-Crosserosis

I've done it again. I was staring at the end of my nose and had my eyes crossed for a long time. And you know what? They got hung up—my eyes, I mean. I couldn't get them uncrossed. It's a serious condition called Eye-Crosserosis. (You can read what big problems Eye-Crosserosis cost me in my second book.) This condition throws everything out of focus, as you can see from the scrambled words below. Can you help me unscramble these words from this book?

1. EOHPCRITEL _____
2. UZABZRD _____
3. OORNCCA _____
4. WOOYBC _____
5. TRGRIGE _____

6. KYIRCT _____
7. OERDRV _____
8. TCNIAPA _____
9. NDSMEAS _____
10. HPOYN _____

"Rhyme Time"

Eddy the Rac decides he's tired of what he's been doing on the ranch. He's going to leave the ranch and find a job. What jobs could he do?

Make a rhyme using the name of Ed that would relate to the jobs below.

1. Ed starts a business to make sleeping spots.

2. Ed develops a new kind of tire.

3. Ed provides the middle writing part for pencils.

4. Ed starts a used bookstore.

5. Ed makes stuff to hold your peanut butter and jelly.

6. Ed writes a book with all his famous quotations.

7. Ed starts a doctor school.

8. Ed makes toys for snowy days.

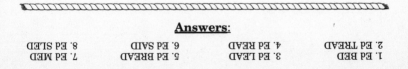

Answers:

1. ED BED   3. ED LEAD   5. ED BREAD   7. ED MED
2. ED TREAD   4. ED READ   6. ED SAID   8. ED SLED

Have you read all of Hank's adventures?

1 *The Original Adventures of Hank the Cowdog*
2 *The Further Adventures of Hank the Cowdog*
3 *It's a Dog's Life*
4 *Murder in the Middle Pasture*
5 *Faded Love*
6 *Let Sleeping Dogs Lie*
7 *The Curse of the Incredible Priceless Corncob*
8 *The Case of the One-Eyed Killer Stud Horse*
9 *The Case of the Halloween Ghost*
10 *Every Dog Has His Day*
11 *Lost in the Dark Unchanted Forest*
12 *The Case of the Fiddle-Playing Fox*
13 *The Wounded Buzzard on Christmas Eve*
14 *Hank the Cowdog and Monkey Business*
15 *The Case of the Missing Cat*
16 *Lost in the Blinded Blizzard*
17 *The Case of the Car-Barkaholic Dog*

18 *The Case of the Hooking Bull*

19 *The Case of the Midnight Rustler*

20 *The Phantom in the Mirror*

21 *The Case of the Vampire Cat*

22 *The Case of the Double Bumblebee Sting*

23 *Moonlight Madness*

24 *The Case of the Black-Hooded Hangmans*

25 *The Case of the Swirling Killer Tornado*

26 *The Case of the Kidnapped Collie*

27 *The Case of the Night-Stalking Bone Monster*

28 *The Mopwater Files*

29 *The Case of the Vampire Vacuum Sweeper*

30 *The Case of the Haystack Kitties*

31 *The Case of the Vanishing Fishhook*

32 *The Garbage Monster from Outer Space*

33 *The Case of the Measled Cowboy*

34 *Slim's Good-bye*

35 *The Case of the Saddle House Robbery*

36 *The Case of the Raging Rottweiler*

37 *The Case of the Deadly Ha-Ha Game*

38 *The Fling*

39 *The Secret Laundry Monster Files*

40 *The Case of the Missing Bird Dog*

41 *The Case of the Shipwrecked Tree*

42 *The Case of the Burrowing Robot*

43 *The Case of the Twisted Kitty*

44 *The Dungeon of Doom*

45 *The Case of the Falling Sky*